Cast of Ch

Emily Bryce. Owner of the Lenten
she's been married to Henry for 28 n
is still going strong. As ditzy as she ᵢ.., ---- .....-.. .. ..-.. ᵖ.........-..

Henry Bryce. Emily's bemused husband (and employee). He humors Emily and keeps her out of the kitchen.

Lincoln "Link" Simpson. The Bryces' best pal, he owns the antique shop on the ground floor of the building where their studio is located.

George Peel. A wealthy English client, who hires Emily to decorate some cabinets for his married daughter, who's setting up a flat in London.

Olivia Palling. His meek daughter, who loathes riding and hunting but lets her husband bully her into doing both.

Roy Palling. Her overbearing husband, whom everybody dislikes.

Miss Ada Birtwistle. Peel's cousin, a tough old bird of 75 who has an iron will and strong opinions on just about everything.

Marie Dennis. Olivia's friend, who seems attracted to Roy. Athletic, assertive, and a bit on the horsey side, she's everything Olivia is not.

Alfredo Vittorio. The flamboyant New York decorator who arranged the Bryces' London commission.

Mr. Jerome. London's top decorator, who worked with Vittorio on the project.

Hilda Leghorn. Emily's best friend, a hairdresser who plans to make her fortune selling nose oil.

Mr. Hedges. A short, square little Englishman with a sandy beard, a derby hat, and an umbrella. He claims to be an antiques dealer.

Roscoe. Emily's devoted but illiterate assistant. She fires him twice a month.

Mr. Gottlieb. The delicatessen owner. He hates being called Fritz.

Sergeant Myron Fisher. A policeman, who puts up with the Bryces.

Plus assorted police, neighbors, clients, and shopkeepers.

Books by Margaret Scherf

Featuring Emily and Henry Bryce
The Gun in Daniel Webster's Bust (1949)
The Green Plaid Pants (1951)
Glass on the Stairs (1954)
The Diplomat and the Gold Piano (1963)

Featuring the Reverend Martin Buell
Always Murder a Friend (1948)
Gilbert's Last Toothache (1949)
The Curious Custard Pie (1950)
The Elk and the Evidence (1952)
The Cautious Overshoes (1956)
Never Turn Your Back (1959)
The Corpse in the Flannel Nightgown (1965)

Featuring Grace Severance
The Banker's Bones (1968)
The Beautiful Birthday Cake (1971)
To Cache a Millionaire (1972)
The Beaded Banana (1978)

Featuring Lieutenant Ryan
The Owl in the Cellar (1945)
Murder Makes Me Nervous (1948)

Nonseries
The Corpse Grows a Beard (1940)
The Case of the Kippered Corpse (1941)
They Came to Kill (1942)
Dead: Senate Office Building (1953)
Judicial Body (1957)
If You Want Murder Well Done (1974)
Don't Wake Me Up While I'm Driving (1977)

For Children
The Mystery of the Velvet Box (1963)
The Mystery of the Empty Trunk (1964)
The Mystery of the Shaky Staircase (1965)

Historical Novel
Wedding Train (1960)

The
Green Plaid
Pants

by Margaret Scherf

Rue Morgue Press
Boulder / Lyons

To
Philena Weller Montgomery

The Green Plaid Pants
0-915230-80-1
Copyright © 1951, 1979
New material copyright © 2005
The Rue Morgue Press

Reprinted with the permission of the author's estate.

The Rue Morgue Press
P.O. Box 4119
Boulder, Colorado 80306
800-699-6214
www.ruemorguepress.com

Printed by
Johnson Printing

PRINTED IN THE UNITED STATES OF AMERICA

About Margaret Scherf

Margaret Scherf was born on April Fools' Day 1908 in Fair-mont, West Virginia. Her father was a high school teacher and the family moved first to New Jersey and then to Wyoming, before finally settling in Montana. After graduation from high school in Cascade, Montana, she attended Antioch College (1925-1928) in Yellow Springs, Ohio, a very small town near Dayton. She left college short of graduation to take a job as an editorial secretary with Robert M. McBride, a book publishing firm located in New York City. Wanderlust struck her in 1929 and she embarked on a round-the-world trip, an experience that would instill in her a love of travel that would stay with her for the rest of her life. Upon her return to the United States, she joined the staff of the Camp Fire Girls national magazine in 1932 (an experience she would put to use in 1948's *Murder Makes Me Nervous*), then moved on to the staff of the Wise Book Company as a secretary and copy-writer in 1934. In 1939, she quit her job and launched her career as a full-time writer, publishing three mysteries with Putnam between 1940 and 1942. With the advent of World War II, she temporarily abandoned her writing career and took a job as secretary to the Naval Inspector, Bethehem Steel Shipyard in Brooklyn.

After the war, she returned to writing and eventually found her-self back in Montana, a state she was to call home for the rest of her life. She continued to revisit New York settings in her books during this period, most notably in the Emily and Henry Bryce series, but her postwar books were primarily set in more rustic locales. "Small town characters, especially Episcopalians, were my delight," she wrote to a critic in 1979.

Chief among those characters was the Reverend Martin Buell, an Episcopalian minister just on the wrong side of middle age who brings both his housekeeper and a "we'll do things my way" attitude to a small Montana parish. Martin's bishop explained that things had been "slipping" in the parish and the parishioners needed a bit of "bullying." He sent the right man. Buell was to ride roughshod over his parishioners during the course of seven books published between 1948 and 1965.

Scherf alternated the Buell books with a daffy series featuring Emily and Henry Bryce, two Manhattan decorators. When we first meet them in 1949's *The Gun in Daniel Webster's Bust*, Emily is pushing Henry to marry him, an idea that doesn't sit too well with him given the fact his last marriage ended when his wife threw a cup of hot coffee in his face. But marry they did, and continued to solve crimes in their own fashion, Emily providing the right-brained, intuitive approach to crime solving while the left-brained Henry relied—more or less—on logic. The Bryce series ended in 1963 after four books.

Her other major series featured Dr. Grace Severance, a retired pathologist. This series, like Scherf herself, moved between Montana and Arizona, beginning with Arizona-based *The Banker's Bones* in 1968 and ending four books later in 1978 with *The Beaded Banana,* set in Montana. The Arizona locale was a familiar one by this time, as Scherf was now spending her winters in Quartzsite, Arizona, a small mining town near the California border, halfway between Phoenix and Las Vegas, Nevada

But she was no longer alone. In 1965, at the age of 57, she surprised friends and relatives by marrying Perry E. Beebe. She helped her husband run a cherry orchard near Yellow Bay, Montana, when she wasn't writing or tending to one of the three antique shops she owned at various times in and around Kalispell. The same year she married Perry the politically outspoken Scherf was also elected as a Democrat to the Montana state legislature. Perry died in 1975 and Peggy moved into a house she had built in Bigfork. On May 12, 1979, she was struck and killed by a drunk driver south of Kalispell.

For more information on Scherf see Tom & Enid Schantz' introduction to The Rue Morgue Press edition of *The Gun in Daniel Webster's Bust.*

Chapter 1

"Henry, do you realize we've been married twenty-eight months and nothing has happened?" Emily dipped her brush and added an eye to the Chinaman she was painting on a coffee table.

"You broke my collarbone——"

"That was an accident."

"The studio caught fire, Di Nobili sued us for eight hundred dollars, Roscoe had chicken pox, your mother lost her diamond pin, and you gained twelve pounds."

"All utter trivia," Emily said, wiping her brush on her smock. "I mean nothing has happened to our marriage."

"I still wonder how you talked me into it." Henry lighted a cigarette and looked down on Lexington Avenue, where a late spring snow was being churned to cocoa by taxis and busses. "I wonder if something will happen in London to liberate me?"

"If London is going to break up our marriage, I'm not going," Emily said firmly.

"You wouldn't miss this trip for a dozen husbands."

"It means absolutely nothing to me." Emily picked up the phone which had been ringing steadily for some minutes. "Hello. Yes, Mrs. Cormorant, he's working on it now. Really. Well, actually we can't let you have it until next week. We're flying to England tonight—for the weekend. Isn't it marvelous? We've been sent for by the biggest decorator in London. Money is no object. It's not our money, of course. I'm going to antique two cabinets for some lord's living room. Henry"—she put her hand over the phone—"will you have that chest done by next Wednesday?" She returned to the phone without waiting for an answer. "Yes, Mrs. Cormorant, he swears by all that's holy you'll get it by Wednesday. Good-by."

"Emily," Henry said sternly, "you know we can't possibly be back in New York by Wednesday, let alone finish up any work."

Emily smiled. "You're so sweet and honest, Henry. I think I'll be sick on the plane, so I'd better not wear my new gabardine suit till I get there."

"Why not go as you are?" Link Simpson asked, coming in with three containers of coffee. He was the owner of Lincoln Simpson's Antique Shop on the ground floor of the building. "I didn't think you'd have time to go out for coffee on this day of days, but I see you've finished all the work so you can leave with a clear conscience." He cast a doleful eye over the tables, chairs, beds, chests, secretaries, sconces, clocks, and other objects which decorators found it profitable to have antiqued by Emily Bryce. Some of these items had been in the studio so long that Emily didn't know who had brought them. Each had been the subject of furious controversy and ingenious fabrication. Emily was incapable of turning down a job.

"I don't expect to make the plane," Henry confessed. "It's four o'clock now."

"We'll make it," Emily said cheerfully. "Is there anything you'd like us to bring you, Link? We're getting some epaulets or something for Vittorio."

Link didn't know of anything. "Just have a good time and see London. And keep your eyes open for smart tricks. I wish you'd got this job from anybody but Alfredo Vittorio."

"I agree," Henry said, beginning to put away his brushes. "He's as slippery as a canned peach."

"You just don't like Alfredo's shirts," Emily objected. "He's all right. Just think, tomorrow morning we'll be having breakfast in bed with the Duke of Orange."

"The man's name is Peel," Henry corrected. "Simply Mr. George Peel."

"Who's going to believe we're flying to London to antique two cabinets for anything less than a duke?"

Roscoe returned from the drugstore where he took his afternoon coffee and reflected on coming catastrophes, such as Emily's flight to London. He had worked for Emily in the Lentement Studio long before she married Henry Bryce, worshiped her, and asked her advice on everything from Cascara to savings banks. Roscoe had only one bad habit—using his own judgment. Emily fired him twice a month.

"So long," Roscoe sighed. "I never see you again." And he took out his comb and arranged his dyed black hair for his homeward subway journey.

"We'll see you on Tuesday," Emily said cheerfully. "Take the mail out of the box and leave it here on the desk, and don't bother answering the phone—it will just be complaints. And be sure to take your pills."

Roscoe agreed mournfully, and they locked the studio. With Link's help they reached La Guardia Field a minute early. Emily wore her gabardine suit, on the theory that you only live once. There was some fuss about the paints and brushes she was carrying under her arm in cardboard boxes, but finally she and her equipment were loaded.

At half-past six the next evening Henry was sipping a glass of whiskey and toasting his feet before the electric grate in their room at the Royal Rajah Hotel in Kensington. He was comfortable, and thoroughly aware of his comfort because it was in marked contrast to what he had been feeling all day. Everyone they had met said it never snowed in London in April. But it was snowing.

A peaceful sound of roaring water came from the bathroom, where Emily planned to restore her circulation by means of a hot bath.

Henry was halfway through his drink when Emily shrieked. He made his way across the icy floor in his stocking feet.

Emily was out of the tub, dripping.

"When I sat down it was over my head!"

"Did you have to fill it to the brim?"

"It's a plot to drown foreigners. Henry, what goes on in these bathrooms? The toilet is named Alerto and the paper is Bronco."

"You have exactly forty minutes to dress."

"Why didn't Lord Peel take us to his manor?"

"Mr. Peel has no manor. He had a house in Marlborough, but he sold it. Taxes too high."

"Then what does he need with a pair of cabinets?"

"He's going to furnish an apartment in London for his daughter." Henry went back to the grate and picked up his glass.

"He's a cute little man," Emily called, splashing. "Nice and pink, with a twinkle in his eye."

Henry grunted. After a while Emily came out and began rooting through her suitcase. "What shall I wear down to the deep-freeze?"

"You brought a dress, didn't you?"

"But it hasn't any sleeves. Oh well, I'll throw your bathrobe around me."

"You'll be a lady, if I have to die in the attempt."

Emily muttered that pneumonia was inevitable and Henry really didn't care about her health and anyone who left home was an idiot, but she put on the backless and frontless black taffeta, drenched herself in Scandale and sat down to work on her fingernails. Henry placed a newspaper under the operation and hoped for the best.

"What do you think of him?" Emily demanded.

"Who?"

"Lord Peel, of course."

"Seems like an amiable chip off the old gentry. Smokes a pipe, hates the government, has a bit of a cold." Henry stretched his feet nearer to the fire. "They say you get chilblains doing this. Peel seems pretty much wrapped up in his daughter."

Emily gave Henry a look. "What do you think of Olivia?"

Henry saw the look. "I think it would be nice if she didn't have a husband."

"Oh, you do. You like that ten cents' worth of God-help-us. A person could read the paper through her. She couldn't run a business."

"She doesn't need to. She has money."

Emily viciously swabbed her thumb with red varnish. "If she has money, why does she stay here?"

"I suppose this was quite a hotel in its day."

"Yes, I imagine the Pilgrim Fathers had a jolly old time here."

Henry considered the Royal Rajah, sipping the rest of his whisky. You would never suspect the interior as you drove up to the imposing marquee, saw the polished brass door handles, the porter's blue-and-gold uniform, and sniffed the atmosphere of extreme gentility which hung about the front steps. Even in the wide hall, which wasn't quite a lobby, you might not be aware that here was a temple to unshakable indifference. The porter's desk had a solid, reassuring look, garnished with keys and pigeonholes for mail. But Mr. Peel said letters to people who had died, and whom the Royal Raj knew had died, remained there for years. Letters to people whose names began with *C*, accidentally getting into slot *R*, remained indefinitely in *R*. Newcomers who didn't know they were expected to inquire of the porter for letters never got their mail at all.

As for the Smithsonian elevator, it was a sacred cow, not to be lightly ridden in. Able-bodied people, Peel said, were obliged to lay down a string from their rooms to the lobby, or feel their way back, up and down narrow red-carpeted stairways, through long tunnels of hall, across glassed-in runways from one building to another, occasionally inquiring the road from an ancient resident.

"I imagine they come here out of habit," Henry said. "The way we go to the bar and grill, even though the food is awful. They like it because the bad service has a personal touch."

"I don't think Olivia fell off her horse," Emily declared, going back to the more controversial subject. "I think she's looking for sympathy."

"She won't get it from that husband of hers," Henry grunted. "Roy Palling is about as sympathetic as internal revenue."

"I think he's cute," Emily countered.

"That big ox?"

"He has charm. You never like men with charm, Henry."

Henry shrugged. He had a feeling that Emily would be all through with Roy, charm or no charm, in about an hour.

They made their way through the halls and down the stairways, came out in a broom closet off the dining room, and were escorted to the cocktail lounge by the headwaiter. Mr. Peel and Roy Palling were warming their rears at a good coal fire and Olivia sat stiffly on a cold, hard, chromium chair. Henry thought she looked quite beautiful, and he could see from Emily's eyebrows that she agreed with him. They were the only customers of the very old and very sad bartender.

"We'll have to hurry on, I'm afraid," Mr. Peel explained. "The residents—these old ladies you see about—demolish everything like a horde of locusts. It's best to be on time." He ordered the drinks, and then there was a silence.

Henry could see Roy Palling stirring around in his brain for something to say. Finally he managed to convey that he considered the weather rather too bad for this time of year.

Mrs. Palling was watching Emily, and it occurred to Henry that she was rather awed by Emily. It also occurred to him that Olivia Palling was afraid of her husband.

Mr. Peel handed a glass to his daughter. "You're sure you ought to be down here?" he asked. "It won't tire you too much?"

"She's perfectly able to sit up and take her dinner with the rest of us," Roy said impatiently. "It wasn't a bad fall."

"I understood you were not there." Mr. Peel turned a heavy eyebrow on his son-in-law.

Olivia looked anxiously from one to the other. "It wasn't a bad fall, Father," she said. "Roy is right. You worry too much about me."

"In any case," her father continued, "there will be no more jumping for you, Olivia. You never did like it. I can't see why you insist on doing something that nearly always results in an injury."

"I suppose it's like eating curried shrimp," Emily put in amiably. "It always makes me sick, but I can't resist it. Remember the time in the Pierre, Henry, when I had to leave the table on the double——"

Henry cut off this reminiscence with a look, and Emily, hurt, turned her attention to the two large sepia prints on the wall behind her. One was entitled "The Happy Mother" and showed a hound with seven pups; the other, called, "Oh for the Touch of a Vanished Hand," showed a less-fortunate hound lying on a glove and looking very gloomy.

They finished their drinks and went into the dining room, where several of the residents Mr. Peel had mentioned were already lapping up the last of their pink blanc mange. For the most part the old ladies sat alone, or with one companion, at small tables, and each was bastioned by a formidable array of bottles and jars of fish paste, anchovy paste, and jam.

"That's Cousin Ada's table," Mr. Peel said, pulling out Emily's chair and nodding to the right. "She's off somewhere, as usual. But you must meet her before you go back—bit of old England, Cousin Ada. Seventy-five and tough as horsehide."

Henry noted that Cousin Ada's table contained none of the little jars.

"It was Cousin Ada who discovered the Royal Rajah, back in the days when it had a bit of swank. Now it's become a family institution and we all stay here when we're in town."

"When our flat is finished, you won't have to come here, dear," Olivia said. "The food is really dreadful."

"I hardly see how we can put up anyone," Roy countered with a smile that made you want to dispose of his teeth.

"But Roy, dear, surely if Father——" She looked quickly at Emily and Henry, smiled. "Isn't it boring to have to listen to family discussions?"

"I'd always rather be in the fight," Emily agreed, and then the waiter, a small pink-and-white rabbit, approached her.

"Thick or clear?" he inquired deferentially.

Mr. Peel explained that this was a way of referring to soup and advised the clear. "Never know what they've put into the cream. We'll all have the boiled chicken, Albert."

Emily asked about the meat pie, and Mr. Peel told her it was a sort of marble slab with imbedded fat and bits of ham and veal framed by a wettish crust.

"Not good enough for an American," Roy put in sourly.

"Not fit for any civilized being," Mr. Peel said, smiling. He seemed determined not to quarrel with Roy, and Henry felt that it would have been a very pleasant evening without Palling. Peel was a comfortable talker with a fund of anecdotes from the chemical business and from their family life in Marlborough. Palling sat back like a hedgehog and gave off occasional disparaging grunts.

Henry finally couldn't resist prodding him. "What do you do for a living, Palling?" he inquired, not too politely.

Roy's lip curled. "I do not paint ladies' boudoirs."

"No? More amusing to visit them?" Henry turned quickly to Peel and asked where they would do the work on the cabinets.

"I want to start early in the morning," Emily warned. "Say about eight o'clock."

"The cabinets are at Jerome's," Mr. Peel said. "But I'm afraid he will not open before ten."

"Mrs. Bryce won't be up before eleven," Henry assured him. "These resolutions are a nightly routine."

"That's very unfair, Henry. These people don't know me at all, and they think you're telling the truth. I want to finish the cabinets tomorrow and see London on Sunday."

Mr. Peel smiled. "You Americans. I'm sure you can't do them in less than a week, Mrs. Bryce. Then you will need another week to look about. We shall be very hurt if you don't see something of our country."

"I'm sure it's a very nice country, but I have to be back Monday. Di Nobili will kill me if his work isn't ready before the end of next week."

"Father," Olivia spoke up quickly, "Mr. Jerome's shop will be closed tomorrow. It's Saturday."

Mr. Peel came up with the suggestion that they move the cabinets to Olivia's flat where Emily could paint whenever it suited her.

"If I know these decorators, the floor will be ruined in the process," Roy remarked.

"Mrs. Bryce is extremely fastidious," Henry lied. "She has done any number of antiquing jobs after the rugs and furnishings were placed in new apartments."

"Thank you, Henry," Emily said gratefully. "Remember the time I fell off the ladder and spilled a bucket of paint on Mrs. Weissman's pink carpet?"

"I don't recall any such incident."

"Oh, Henry, you do. First I threw a newspaper over the spot, then I fainted because I had turned my ankle, and when I came to nobody had discovered it yet, so I went into the bathroom and found a razor and I shaved the paint right off the carpet and walked on it a little and you couldn't see a thing."

Olivia went to her room immediately after the cheese and biscuits but Roy lingered, stretching his insolent big feet to the fire in the drawing room and absorbing the venomous looks of various old ladies about the room without seeming to notice.

"I've been thinking," Roy said, addressing Mr. Peel and shutting out Emily and Henry, "that a trip to America might do Olivia a great deal of good. She takes these mishaps far too seriously."

"I am under the impression you force her to do this practice jumping," Mr. Peel replied. "Olivia has never cared for hunting. She must give it up before she kills herself."

"Nonsense. Everyone's got to take his share of spills. She loves it, really."

"She hates it." Mr. Peel jammed tobacco into his pipe with short, sharp thrusts, slapped his pocket, located a matchbox, and sternly inhaled. "Must give it up. Do you hear?"

"I still say hunting is good for Olivia. It gives her a sense of power. She needs to feel herself master of something."

"Why?" Mr. Peel demanded.

"It's a fundamental human need."

"Who says so?"

"All the psychologists."

"Pfah!" Mr. Peel sat back angrily.

"Perhaps we could secure passage on your ship, Bryce," Roy suggested.

"We flew over."

"Oh." Roy frowned. "I distrust flying."

"You ought to do more of it," his father-in-law told him. "Gives one a sense of power."

"Wouldn't consider taking a ship back, I suppose?" Roy continued, still addressing Henry.

"I would, but Emily is not a good sailor."

"We can't afford the time," Emily added.

Mr. Peel seemed pleased that they would not accommodate themselves to Roy. Henry wondered why Roy wanted to attach himself to them in any case. Then he remembered that the English had to land without money. It was undoubtedly convenient to be with an American.

Henry could see that Emily was anxious to go to bed and read some of her crime literature, so they said good night. Mr. Peel came up with them, muttering about the dark halls. "I'm fond of the place, I've come here for so many years. Of course it doesn't suit Roy at all. Here—we go down this passageway and up the other stairs. Shorter." He led the way through a sitting room where no one ever sat, down a dark connecting hall, up two steps, turned to the right, down another passageway, turned to the left, up two more steps, and halted before number 35. The number next to it was 102.

"Roy and Olivia have the room next to yours. I'm on the floor above, in 93," Mr. Peel said. "If you want anything please rap on my door. I'm a light sleeper. Probably shan't turn in until one or thereabouts in any case. I read."

"You do?" Emily beamed. "So do I. If you want to borrow my magazines——"

"I'm sure," Henry cut her off, "Mr. Peel has plenty of reading matter of his own."

"On the contrary, I'd be delighted to see your American literature."

Emily darted into their room and came out with *Inside Detective*. Mr. Peel regarded it with some amazement. The cover showed the practically nude upper half of a young female being choked to death with a pair of fiendish hands.

"This number is a little tame," Emily apologized. "But if you're not used to it you may think it's good. Do you have any English ones to lend me?"

"Nothing like this, I'm afraid," he said sadly. "Can you sleep after you've read it?"

"Oh yes. Sometimes I have nightmares. When I dream that I'm planning to murder Henry I give them up for a week."

Mr. Peel retired, holding the magazine somewhat gingerly by the corner.

Emily shivered as they entered their vast chamber. "Close the windows and turn on the toaster," she begged. "This fresh air will be the death of me."

"Windows in England move only one way, my dear—up. Get into bed. There's probably a hot-water bottle."

Emily promptly followed this advice. "Why, Henry, there is! How did you know?"

"Intuition. Aren't you taking off your clothes?"

"Not till I get back to Sixty-second Street. Hand me my coat, will you?"

Henry tossed it to her and turned on the small electric heater, which glowed like a candle in the catacombs.

Emily read for ten minutes. "It's terribly quiet here. I suppose nobody ever drops a bottle out of a window or beats his wife."

"I like it," Henry said. "It's peaceful." He settled in the armchair before the heater and lighted a cigarette.

"Aren't you going to read or anything? How can you just sit like that, not uttering a sound?"

"I wonder why Olivia married that fat ass," Henry muttered.

"You always wonder why women marry the men they do. Instead of you."

"If I'd been here at the time, undoubtedly it wouldn't have happened."

Emily returned to her printed orgies. There was silence for fully three minutes. "I'm going mad," she announced. "Make a noise, Henry."

"Shh." He got up, moved softly in his stocking feet to the heavy curtain which hung over the locked door to the next room, put his ear to the keyhole. The voice was Roy's.

"Yes, dear, but why did you fall off?" he was saying. "It wasn't a bad jump. When I talked to Marie on the phone just now she said she didn't see why you fell. What was the reason?"

"I don't know, Roy. I don't know."

"You were afraid, I suppose. You're always afraid."

She began to cry softly. "I don't want ever to ride again."

"Nonsense. You've got to conquer this absurd fear. There's no real danger so long as you're not a coward."

"People do get killed."

"You'll have to hunt in the fall, when we visit the Penningtons."

"Roy, no. Please don't keep talking about it. I never want to ride again."

"Best way to cure it, my dear. Unless you want everyone to say you're a coward. Do you want them to say that?"

"I know I'm a coward. I can't conceal it from people, Roy. And the poor horse."

"He'd never have fallen on the stake if you hadn't pulled up in a fright. Damned good horse, and we shall have to pay for him, you know. One shouldn't go about killing good horses and spilling their insides on the ground."

"Oh, Roy, please!" Olivia begged.

Henry let the curtain fall and came back to his chair. "The dirty bastard," he said softly. "The dirty bastard."

"What's going on in there?"

"He's torturing her."

Emily looked at the cold floor and then at the curtained doorway. "I wish we had a dictaphone or a wire recorder or something." She slid out of bed and took up the listening. "She's a dope," Emily said in a loud whisper. "Why doesn't she kick his teeth in? All she does is cry. I can't stand women who cry."

Henry told her to be quiet, but she went on listening and making suggestions. "It must be his money or she wouldn't stick to him, Henry. Or does she like him? You never know. Look at me."

"Look at you. Get back in bed; they'll hear your teeth chattering."

"They don't mean anything to me. Let them hear me."

Chapter 2

As Henry had anticipated, Emily could not be roused next morning until after ten. The dining room had officially closed, but Mr. Peel had it reopened, headwaiter and all.

"Where are the silver salvers?" Emily demanded, looking about the dark room at the small tables.

"Don't mind her," Henry told the uneasy headwaiter. "She thinks England should be a combination of broiled kidneys and Arthur Treacher." He hurried her through breakfast—no great trick, as Emily didn't care for kipper and fried tomatoes.

With Mr. Peel they found a cab and arrived at the flat, where Jerome was waiting. Henry disliked Jerome at once, but Emily appeared to accept him as just another decorator, one of a strange breed. He had a weary and condescending manner, but so had a dozen of the New York gentry. He went into great detail as to how the two old mahogany cabinets were to be antiqued. Then he took a note from his pocket.

"Vittorio writes me," he said, "that he would like a pair of Franz Joseph epaulets, if you don't mind taking them back with you."

"I don't mind," Emily told him. "He asked me about it."

"I shall stop on Monday to see what progress you have made," he said finally, and taking his samples of brocade departed.

"I'll be all through on Monday," Emily told Mr. Peel, "but I didn't tell him because you can't get much done with decorators hanging over you. This is going to be a nice little place when you get it fixed up," she added, glancing at the white marble fireplace and the tall windows.

"Did Roy hire Jerome?" Henry asked abruptly.

"No, as a matter of fact I did."

"It's Mr. Peel's money," Emily put in bluntly. "He probably wants to see how it's spent." She began spreading newspapers on the floor. "Get the cans open, Henry. Where's the turpentine? Where's my big brush? Let's not stand around all day. Where can I put on my clothes?"

She went into the next room to change, and Henry explained to Mr. Peel that Emily always scolded everyone else when she was late.

"I expect Roy will be along later in the day," Mr. Peel remarked, looking into space.

"I suppose he wants to see how things shape up." Henry tied on his apron and began prying open the cans.

"Roy's not a bad sort, really," Mr. Peel went on, more as if he were trying to convince himself than Henry. "Never had to do any hard work, you know. That isn't good for a man."

"His father had money?"

"Yes. Didn't leave Roy a great deal, though. Death duties consumed most of the estate. Damned government." He said this more as a habitual oath than as a matter he was presently concerned with. "Roy has sat at various desks in various law firms. Never heard of his handling a case. But he's not a bad sort. I have nothing to complain of."

Henry felt that Mr. Peel wanted to tell somebody what he really thought of his son-in-law. If he had been on the point of telling Henry, he was prevented by the return of Emily, who held up a pair of red-and-green plaid trousers with feet.

"What on earth are these?" she demanded.

"Oh, those. A bit of an heirloom from the house in Marlborough," Mr. Peel told her. "Those trousers were worn by Bonnie Prince Charlie during his flight. He shed them and put on a pair given him by a kind lady who wished to aid the Stuart cause."

"You mean Charlie was trying to hide out in red-and-green pants? They could have got a bead on him at twenty miles."

"Gay plaids were the style, I presume." Mr. Peel smiled.

"Where are the pants she gave him in exchange for the ones he gave her?"

"That I don't know. Perhaps in a museum somewhere."

Emily shook her head. "And I always thought he was a man women fell for."

Emily started work with that look of bright concentration she had when she was painting. Her mouth stayed open, and her answers to Mr. Peel were monosyllabic.

The old gentleman was content to sit on a packing case and watch them. As Emily said later, he seemed to regard them as his private imports from America and he wanted to get the most out of the experience.

At one o'clock the bell rang and Mr. Peel let in a very tall, very gaunt woman with an iron chin, a searching eye, an umbrella, and a hearing aid. He introduced her as his cousin, Miss Ada Birtwistle.

"Miss Ada has twenty or thirty cousins and friends whom she visits in the country," he explained. "We never know where to find her."

"There's no need for you to find me," Miss Birtwistle said practically. "If I die, you will be notified. Otherwise you may assume I am in reasonable health."

Emily told Henry to bring her a chair. "Tell me about England, Miss Birtwistle," she said.

"England?" Miss Birtwistle dismissed the whole country with a shrug, and turned to her cousin. "George, do you know that people are actually buying that dreadful horny tropical fruit—pineapple, I believe they call it—at eleven and six? I witnessed such a purchase with my own eyes not ten minutes ago in Oxford Street."

"Don't you like pineapple?" Emily asked.

"The stuff has no taste. I'm sure it cannot be good for them. Can't think what they see in it. George, are Olivia and Roy going to America?"

Mr. Peel took the pipe from his mouth. "Did Olivia tell you they were?"

"No. You know Olivia never decides anything. Roy told me. His excuse is that the trip will be good for Olivia, but I shouldn't be surprised if he had something else in mind."

Miss Birtwistle suddenly undid her hinges and rose from the chair so that she might inspect Emily's work. "George," she said severely, "is this one of the dining-room cabinets from Marlborough?"

Mr. Peel admitted that it was.

"And what, may I ask, is this woman doing to it?"

"The young people like the new ideas in decoration," Mr. Peel told her soothingly. "You can't blame them—they've lived with these old pieces for years. They want a change."

"Change is all very well, but when it comes to blobbing paint all over a good mahogany cabinet, I think someone who has not completely gone out of her mind should call a halt." She had a menacing grip on her umbrella.

Emily saved herself by giving Miss Birtwistle an innocent smile. "You'll like it as time goes on. It will look just like porphyry when I get through."

"I do not approve of things that look like something else. What is suddenly wrong with mahogany?"

"It's all in the point of view." Emily shrugged.

"Was this Roy's idea?"

"Not really. We put the whole job in Mr. Jerome's hands, Ada."

"And how did this Jerome get hold of you? He cannot be any-one of consequence."

"He's well known in the decorating line," Peel said.

"Oh yes," Emily helped him. "Vittorio told us he was the top decorator in London."

"And who is Vittorio?" Miss Ada asked with scorn.

"He's a New York decorator."

"What does an Italian in America know about furnishing an Englishman's house? But it's none of my business. If Olivia and Roy go to New York, I shall go along."

Mr. Peel made a startled noise. "Whatever for?"

"I have the money. I should like to see cowboys and central heating." She turned abruptly toward the door. "I can't waste the afternoon in idle talk." She was gone.

Mr. Peel breathed deeply. "Ada is a bit trying."

"I think she's cute," Emily said. "You know exactly what she's thinking."

"Undoubtedly," her cousin agreed. "She's terribly fond of Olivia. I don't know whether she's more formidable as an enemy or as a friend. She once beat an inland revenue man over the head with her umbrella. She has also been known to call on Roy and Olivia at breakfast time. I'm sure she hopes to catch them in a quarrel."

"Doesn't she like Roy?"

"Afraid not. But it would have been the same with any man Olivia chose to marry. No one is quite good enough for her favorite. The old girl has a bit of change, you know. She'd like to leave it to Olivia, but she hates to think of Roy getting any of it." Mr. Peel stopped suddenly, and Henry thought he wished he hadn't said quite so much.

"Emily, you're getting paint on the floor," Henry scolded. "I told you we ought to use canvas."

"Oh, phooey." Emily bent over and rubbed the spots with a rag. "Is divorce easy in England?"

Before anyone had to deal with that question the door opened and Roy and Olivia came in.

"It's just like Lexington Avenue," Emily said happily. "Everybody who has nothing to do drops in at the studio. So far, though, nobody has brought me any coffee."

Mr. Peel immediately took this errand upon himself.

"Isn't it fascinating?" Olivia sat down to watch Emily. She had a greenish-white look this afternoon that indicated very little sleep and no lunch. "I think you're terribly clever, Mrs. Bryce."

"Nothing clever about it," Roy said. "It's a trade one learns, like any other."

The look Emily gave him should have left nothing of Roy but a little dust to put in an urn. If there was anything Emily firmly believed in it was her own cleverness and the special and unique quality of her work. She was quite justified in her pride, because there was no one in New York who could equal her.

Roy didn't notice the look. "I've been inquiring about air reservations," he said to Henry. "You people have any idea which day you'll be returning to New York?"

"I should think Thursday or Friday," Henry said.

"We're leaving on Tuesday," Emily corrected.

"You won't finish those things before Thursday, dear."

"I'll finish them Monday if I have to work thirty hours a day."

Roy wanted to know if Jerome had been in, and then he said, casually, "I understand you're taking back some sort of curio for him?"

"Epaulets," Henry agreed.

"Has he given them to you?"

"Not yet," Henry answered.

"I wish Mr. Jerome would not make the walls purple," Olivia remarked wistfully. "I've never cared for purple."

"They call it puce," Emily told her. "They're all using it in New York. They say it drives people mad."

"Choose your own wall color, Mrs. Palling," Henry urged. "Mustn't be afraid of these fellows."

"I say if you're paying a man to do a flat you ought to let him do it," Roy pronounced heavily. "Olivia has no taste. She wants everything to look as pink and cozy as Mother Goose."

"I know it's much smarter to have dark colors, but they do depress me terribly," Olivia confessed.

"You're very easily depressed," Roy retorted. "Comes of living indoors all the while. What you need is fresh air and exercise."

"Do you think so?" Emily asked, holding her dripping brush in midair. "I hate fresh air and exercise."

"You do?" Olivia gave her a delighted smile. "I've never heard anyone say that."

"Mrs. Bryce is an American," Roy reminded her.

"I think I shall like America."

Roy looked at his watch. "Time to start for Paddington. Marie's train will be in half an hour."

"Do you mind if I don't go?" Olivia asked. "I'm so tired."

"Just as you wish, my dear."

Henry thought Roy was quite satisfied to meet Marie alone, but he said to his wife as he left, "She's really your friend, you know."

"Who is Marie?" Emily asked as soon as Roy had shut the door.

"A friend from Gloucester. We knew each other as children."

"Does she like fresh air?" Emily asked.

"Oh yes. Marie is a wonderful rider. I hated having her see me fall yesterday."

Mr. Peel came back with the coffee and then he took Olivia away with him, leaving Emily and Henry alone.

"Henry, I don't think Roy and Olivia are happy together," Emily said gravely, crumpling an empty cigarette package.

Henry smiled and went on applying green undercoat.

"Why doesn't she give him the air?"

"She likes him, in a grisly way. Some women like to be tortured, you know."

"Dopes. Maybe when she gets to New York the worm will turn."

"I don't think so. She's much too timid to question Roy, or her father, or even Cousin Ada."

"But Roy and her father are on opposite sides of the ring."

"Did you think Roy showed an unusual interest in the epaulets?"

Emily hadn't noticed. People were often fascinated by the junk that dealers gathered here and there. "You know what I'd like to take back?" she asked. "Charlie's pants." She picked them up and held them around Henry's stomach. "You could wear them on Halloween to frighten the neighbors."

Henry thought perhaps Mr. Peel would give them to Emily, if she hinted.

Emily worked well all afternoon, announced immediately after dinner that she had seen enough of England, and went up to bed to read and keep warm.

Henry found a deep chair with a high back in the rear lounge, where there were not so many of the elderly female residents. Some of them were amiable enough, but others appeared to regard him as an intruder from a country which had plenty of its own coal, and he felt safer at a distance from them. He selected a bound volume of the *Windsor* magazine for the year 1907 and read an article on decorated bicycles. One of the pictures showed Mr. Arthur Thomas's "Sunflower Design" at the Portmadoc Cycling Carnival. Mr. Thomas was wearing a sunflower hat which he had obviously made for himself, and a walrus mustache, which nature had kindly given him.

Presently Henry realized that he was not reading but listening. The voices were those of Roy and Marie, who probably couldn't see him through the aspidistra and primula on the table between. He thought of getting up, and then he argued that as this was a public sitting room he had a perfect right to listen to anything that might offer.

"I don't see how she fell. She had a good mount. There was nothing to the jump—any half-wit could have made it."

Marie answered in her heavy, husky voice, "Olivia detests riding. I can't think why she does it."

"But you like to see her do it, don't you? You want her to break her neck, Marie. You were close to her when she fell."

"Yes, I was." Marie's tone was defensive.

"You willed her to fall. One can, you know. A strong-willed person can force Olivia to do almost anything. You willed her to fall."

"I think you're utterly detestable, Roy. You know I'm fond of Olivia."

"Yes, of course. Old friends and all that rot." His tone as he said these things was not disagreeable. One would have thought, not hearing the words, that he was making amiable conversation.

Henry didn't try to see them. He had a good picture of Marie Dennis, whom he had met at dinner. An honest, direct face, brilliant blue eyes, a splendid physique—probably ate oatmeal and apples every day. A little on the horsy side, perhaps. Very proud of her thick red hair. Dressed plainly but in good tailored wool. But her mind, Henry decided, was not nearly so vigorous as her body. She was definitely under Roy's spell.

"I'm still hungry," she remarked. "What ghastly food they have here."

"You needn't stay here, you know. There are other hotels, with better meals."

"I suppose so. Couldn't we go out and have something? Really, I'm famished."

"Where would you like to go? I expect we shall fare better in America."

"America?" Marie repeated. "Roy, you haven't made up your mind—"

"I understand there is plenty of good food in the United States. One's patience gives out, you know."

"But Roy, you haven't mentioned this until now. When did you decide?" Marie's voice was full of excitement.

"Yesterday. Olivia needs a change. She's all keyed up over this accident."

"Olivia." There was a silence.

"Scott's have a fairly decent late supper," Roy remarked. "Care to wander over there?"

"No, thank you. I'm not hungry now. Shall you be gone long?"

"Remember old Dickie Hornby? I saw him in Regent Street this afternoon. Old Dickie has developed an enormously fat belly. Bald too. I wouldn't have known him."

"Perhaps it would be nice at Scott's," Marie decided.

"What a restless creature you are. Sure this time?"

"Yes. Come along."

"Old Dickie was giving me a long tale about some girl who ran off with another woman's husband. Dirty business. I shouldn't have any respect for a girl who conducted herself in that way, should you?" Roy yawned audibly, and the chair creaked as he got out of it. "Where's your coat?"

Marie changed her mind again. She wasn't hungry, really, she said. She thought she would go up to bed.

"Very well. You're in 73 again, I suppose? Beastly cold room, that."

They left together, and Henry got up, looked around, and saw Miss Birtwistle reading a copy of *True Court Cases* in the corner farthest from the fire.

Emily was in bed with two coats on, sneezing into Kleenex.

"Roy is a number-one heel," he announced.

"Did you just discover that? Marie is his girlfriend, isn't she?"

"She'd like to be," Henry said thoughtfully, "and yet she's the kind of girl who would be ashamed, too, if you know what I mean."

"No, I don't. Either you play around or you don't play around."

"Marie is the strong, wholesome type, but that doesn't mean she isn't attracted by men. Roy is busy teasing her."

"He bores me," Emily said. "They must be awfully short of men here."

"I think it's quite clever the way he works on each of them in the way that will hurt most. By the way, Miss Birtwistle is reading a strange piece of literature. Can't imagine where she got it."

"Henry, I'm tired of England," Emily announced.

"You haven't seen any of it. Perhaps we can take tomorrow off and go into the country."

"The country!" she wailed. "What is there to see in the country?"

"Grass."

"I can see grass in Mama's yard in Babylon. I'm worried about Roscoe. Suppose he dyes his hair again while we're over here?"

"Suppose he does? Roscoe's been dyeing his hair for years."

"Someday he's going to poison himself with that shoe blacking. Or he may set fire to the studio. Or throw Hilda Leghorn out the window onto Lexington Avenue, with a lot of people going by who might see him do it."

Chapter 3

Emily had not, of course, been able to finish the cabinets on Monday. It was late afternoon on Thursday when she finally applied the dust and flyspecks, and Jerome had a photographer in to preserve their likeness for posterity. As soon as the photographer had finished, Jerome was to take Henry, Emily, and Mr. Peel to dinner.

"Barbarous," Miss Ada said. "Deliberate flyspecks!"

"It's all in the point of view," Emily explained, unruffled. "Take radio. I don't like your radio, it's too refined. Ours is more down-to-earth—you know, things that happen to everybody."

"Yes," Henry agreed, "like having an illegitimate child or pushing your grandfather into a vat of molten steel."

"Good enough for most grandfathers," Miss Ada countered, getting up from the packing case where she had been sitting. "I must be off to claim my ticket."

"You really intend to go to America?" Mr. Peel asked, breaking off with Jerome and the photographer. "Do you think that's wise, Cousin Ada?"

"You'll be glad to have me along. I shall sell my Pennsylvania Railroad shares. You have no resources in America, now have you, George?"

Peel blinked at that. "You don't think I'm going?"

"Peters told me you had a reservation. The advantage of having relatives in various offices is that one's movements are as private as the reproductive activities of Rita Hayworth."

"I rather thought I'd surprise you," Peel admitted. "I see I was mistaken."

Henry was not pleased with this development. It would have been a nice party without Palling, but it was apparently Palling's decision to fly to America that had caused Peel and Miss Ada to make similar plans. They were determined to keep him in sight. What was Roy up to?

Jerome handed Henry a small oblong package. "These are the epaulets for Mr. Vittorio," he explained.

"And I have a small gift for Mrs. Bryce," Peel announced, holding up the red-and-green plaid trousers.

"You're giving me Charlie's pants? Oh, how sweet!" Emily cried.

Miss Ada sniffed. "What on earth could one do with those moth-eaten relics?"

"They're an item of great historic interest," Henry told her, winking. "Genuine, original, and authentic."

"I doubt it. Probably a copy of the ones in Edinburgh Castle. Originally the property of my family."

"Won't matter to Emily," Henry assured her, stuffing the trousers into his overcoat pocket. "She'll give them an honored place in her old-glass china closet along with the buffalo skull and the broken fountain pens."

"By the way," Peel said thoughtfully, "I'd appreciate it if you did not mention this to Roy. He's apt to feel that anything from the old place in Marlborough should go to Olivia. Not that these have any monetary value—but you understand how it is."

Miss Ada departed, and shortly after Henry and Emily went to dinner with Mr. Peel and Jerome. It was an excellent meal, and it cost Jerome a nice piece of change. Emily couldn't understand it.

"Decorators at home don't feed you," she said, as they came into the lobby of the Royal Rajah.

"British hospitality," Henry suggested. "Jerome's a smooth customer."

"He reminds me of a wanted-dead-or-alive poster."

Peel laughed. "I assure you Mr. Jerome is a man of sound reputation. Otherwise I shouldn't have allowed him in Olivia's flat with all her things." He went on up to bed.

Henry and Emily wandered into the drawing room, where they found Roy, Marie, and Olivia seated near the fire. Emily threw her coat and the package from Jerome into one chair and herself into another.

Olivia's eyes were bright and feverish, and Marie was trying to make her go to bed. "You won't be fit to travel, darling," she pleaded.

"I couldn't sleep—I'm too excited. Imagine Cousin Ada storming around New York!"

"Yes, imagine it." Roy irritably flipped a cigarette into the fire. "The old girl might have chosen some other week in the last eighty years to visit the Western Hemisphere."

At that moment Miss Ada herself came in, brisk and laden with brown-paper parcels. "The things people give one!" she said indignantly. "Cough medicine, knee warmers, dull books about vicars. Why must one suddenly, after passing seventy, take an interest in vicars? Not one of them ever did anything worth reading about. I shall give the lot to the downstairs man. Olivia, if they have kipper in the morning, I shouldn't recommend your taking it."

"Oh, I shan't take it, Cousin Ada. I can't bear kipper."

"There is nothing wrong with kipper on a sound stomach. However, before an excursion by airplane I consider a boiled egg preferable."

Emily and Henry said good night and went upstairs. It wasn't until she was completely undressed that Emily remembered her coat on the chair in the lounge. "The package from Jerome is there too," she said.

Henry went down to get them. There was no one around but the night porter, and he had Emily's coat in his little cage near the elevator.

"Wasn't there a package too?" Henry asked.

"No, sir. Nothing but the lady's coat, sir."

Emily couldn't understand it. "I know I had that parcel when I came in tonight, Henry."

"I don't know what the night porter would want with a pair of epaulets."

"It's lucky I put Charlie's pants in your overcoat pocket—he'd have taken those too." She continued to fuss about it until she fell asleep. Henry put the shoes outside the door and turned off the heater.

He was worrying about the details of departure and trying to get his bed warm when he thought he heard someone outside the door.

Burton, the downstairs man, didn't come along to do the shoes until early morning, so it wasn't Burton.

Henry took his feet from the hot-water bottle and placed them on the floor, padded to the door, turned the large key, looked into the hall. It was very dark, and he didn't notice for a moment that Emily's shoes were gone. There was no one in sight, and the three visible doors were closed. There was, however, a light in the bathroom. He decided to wait. No one could stay indefinitely in one of those little shrines to pioneer plumbing.

At the end of ten minutes he revised his judgment. There was no sound from the place. Perhaps the light had been left on by mistake. He crept down the hall and tried the door. It was locked.

He returned to his room, noisily closed the door, silently reopened it. The light went out in the bathroom and the figure of Miss Birtwistle, shrouded in flowered flannel and crowned with curlers, moved majestically into the hall, paused to peer up and down, went on to her own room. She was not, Henry was positive, carrying anything whatever.

Oh well, he thought, perhaps old Burton had taken Emily's shoes away to do a special job. He had taken a great liking to Emily, and he was "a bit mental," as Miss Ada called it.

Henry shrugged and returned to the hot-water bottle.

In the morning both pairs of shoes were at the door. So was an oblong package tied with brown cord, unmistakably the one from Jerome.

"The porter opened this and decided he didn't need epaulets," Henry said. "Will you kindly get out of bed, Mrs. Bryce, and clothe yourself?"

Emily turned over, stretched, and smiled. "We're going home, Henry," she sighed. "Isn't it wonderful? I feel as if I'd been away for years."

"You will be if we don't make that plane. Reservations don't grow on every bush, my pet. Old Burton will be sorry to see you go. He's polished your shoes down to the lining." He dropped them on her chest.

"He's a sweet old man. I wonder how he'd get along with Roscoe in the studio."

"He wouldn't. Don't get any ideas about importing slave labor.

It's enough that you mesmerize me into working for a necktie a month."

This remark went unchallenged. Emily was examining the heels of her shoes. "The lifts are crooked, Henry. Look."

He looked. "You'd almost think someone had taken them off and nailed them on again."

"What do you mean, almost? Mr. Burton must be practicing to open a repair shop."

Henry took the shoes to the table and with the aid of his pocket knife and a bottle opener removed the lifts. "Hmm," he muttered.

This got Emily out of bed. "What's so interesting?" she demanded, leaning on his shoulder. "Henry, they've been digging holes in my shoes!"

Someone had taken an awl and made a small hole in each wooden heel. "I don't get it," Henry admitted. "Something screwy."

"I'm glad I didn't have them on," Emily decided. "Who says the Americans are crazy? Don't stand there all day. Put the heels back on, Henry. We've got to catch a plane."

It was too early for the residents to be at breakfast when they came down. They found Mr. Peel alone in the dining room, eating fried plaice.

"The others are breakfasting in their rooms," he said. "I hope you had a good night?"

"Somebody took my shoes apart," Emily told him, removing the cap from the anchovy sauce and sniffing.

"What was that about your shoes, Mrs. Bryce?" Peel asked.

Emily gave him a complete description. Mr. Peel looked carefully at his plate, wiped his mouth with his napkin, and remarked that it was odd, very odd indeed.

"Burton's pretty old and a little off," Henry suggested. "He may have been curious about the way American shoes are made."

"Quite so." Peel still didn't look up.

Emily, meanwhile, had gone to the next table and returned with a pill bottle and a small jar of fish paste. "I've been dying to find out what's in these jars and bottles," she confessed. "These old ladies live to be over a hundred and meaner than John L. Sullivan, and all they take besides what I eat is this stuff in jars."

She swallowed a couple of the pills and spread some of the

paste on a piece of Mr. Peel's toast. Judging from her expression it was not particularly tasty.

"I'd rather die in the full flower of my youth," she decided. "We almost lost Mr. Jerome's epaulets last night, but they came back this morning."

Peel gave her a puzzled smile. "You seem to have had your troubles during the night. How did you lose the epaulets?"

Emily told him she had left them in the lounge on a chair, and in the morning they were at the door. "The porter said he hadn't seen them at all," she added.

"So long as you don't mislay Prince Charlie's trousers," Peel said lightly. "I shouldn't like to think of their finding their way to some ignoble dustbin."

What they could see of the weather between the red plush curtains looked unpromising, so Henry called the airport. Flight postponed, they said. Emily fumed. She hated waiting around.

"I'll take you to the silver vaults in Chancery Lane," Mr. Peel suggested soothingly. "You'll enjoy it ever so much, and perhaps you'll find something you like."

Henry decided to remain at the hotel. He felt that Emily would be brought back in good time by Mr. Peel, and after last night he wanted to keep an eye on their luggage. He kept in touch with the airport, and at eleven, when Peel telephoned, the report was still unfavorable. Peel said he and Mrs. Bryce would have lunch at Scott's, in that case, and Henry said fine. He would have gone out himself, to avoid the veal-and-ham pie, if it hadn't been for Palling. That gentleman had hung about all morning, and twice Henry had come into the hall and found him leaning over the porter's desk, studying the mound of luggage and wraps awaiting their departure. Roy had straightened quickly each time, said something about the boredom of waiting about, and sauntered into the drawing room.

After a while Emily and Mr. Peel came back from their expedition. "Henry, you should have been there!" Emily cried. "Mountains of old silver soup ladles! Look what Mr. Peel bought me." She tore the paper and string from a Sheffield coffeepot, with a strawberry on the lid for a knob.

"Very generous of you, Peel," Henry said. "Ought not to have

given her anything so handsome—she's bound to leave it somewhere, you know."

"It's an inexpensive one. Mrs. Bryce liked it and I thought she
ought to have it. Little mark of appreciation for her excellent work."

They had a light supper and then there was a great confusion of
people, luggage, paintbrushes, and tickets. Olivia wanted to say
good-by to Marie, but no one could find Marie. At last Miss Ada,
Mr. Peel, the Pallings, and the Bryces were disposed in two cabs.
There was a bus trip after that, and a great deal of business with
passports and currency, and then Henry found himself looking down
on the vanishing lights of England.

Emily had to talk to everyone on the plane. To Emily an
uninterviewed passenger was like melting ice cream—something
had to be done immediately to save it. She wanted to know what
they all did for a living and how many wives they had had.

"You must come and see us," she would say. "Our New York
apartment is too small, but a friend of ours has a beautiful new
country place near Waterfall, in Putnam County. Simpson is the
name, Link Simpson."

Henry protested. "You can't invite people to Link's place."

"Nobody ever takes these invitations seriously," Emily assured
him.

"I hope you're right. You've given them the impression it's an
estate with four butlers."

"What's the difference, if they're not coming? It makes a good
impression."

Henry opened his pigskin bag. "You take charge of Charlie's
pants," he said firmly. "I'm not going through customs with anything so fantastic."

"But I haven't room, Henry."

"Make room. They're your property." He stuffed them into her
dressing case, put the case on the rack overhead.

Emily decided to sleep, and Henry looked about for someone to
talk to. Miss Ada had a seat to herself directly in back of them, but
she was slumming in one of Emily's magazines. Roy and Olivia,
across the aisle, were talking in careful tones. Mr. Peel, however,
sitting alone farther back, looked as if he would welcome company. Henry joined him, and they smoked amiably and discussed

taxes and governments and Peel said it was too bad we had to have either.

Miss Ada took a dressing case off the rack and made her way to the washroom. She was gone a long time.

"Do you think Miss Ada is all right?" Henry asked after a while.

"Oh yes. Tough as an old rooster," Mr. Peel said. "Ought to have been a policeman. Spends most of her life keeping other members of the family in line. She doesn't credit one of us with an ounce of brains. In fact, she still treats me as if I were five years old. Here she comes. I told you she was all right."

Miss Ada stalked back to her seat, put the toilet case on the rack, pulled the rug over her sharp knees, and returned to *How I Killed My Husband in Six Installments*.

Henry, listening to Mr. Peel, was vaguely aware of a disturbing factor in these operations. For a moment he didn't know what it was. Then he realized that Miss Ada had placed Emily's case on the rack. Her own was an archaic affair of alligator, lying next to Mr. Peel's Gladstone. Miss Ada must have taken Emily's case into the washroom. Odd thing to do. Perhaps she was beginning to be absentminded.

The United States customs was somewhat amused by the pants, particularly as Emily said they were her great-grandfather's winter pajamas. The official spent a moment examining the epaulets, asked what they were going to do with them.

"We're in the decorating business," Emily said sweetly. "You know how decorators are."

The man smiled, said okay, Mrs. Bryce, put stickers on everything, and dismissed them.

Their British friends had not been cleared as yet, so Henry took Emily up to the bar for coffee.

"Here we fly all the way in from London," Emily complained, pouring sugar into her cup, "and not even a garbage man to meet us. It's an awful letdown. I think I'll call Link."

Henry said Link would be up in the country on a Saturday morning. Emily borrowed all his change and went to a phone booth. He watched her absently as he drank his coffee, but he was thinking about the four people who had come with them. There was something going on. Very few English traveled these days, and for four of them suddenly to pick up and fly to New York on a few days' notice was highly unusual if not damned suspicious. Something was bubbling, and although he liked Olivia and her father, and had become quite attached to Miss Ada, still he was content that he would see no more of them.

Emily was waving to him from the booth. "Link wants to talk to you," she said as he came over. "He's invited all of us up for the weekend. Isn't he sweet?"

"All of us? All of who?" Henry took the phone. "Hello, Link. What's she talked you into?"

"Emily says you've got a flock of fascinating dukes and lords with you. What time do you figure you'll get here?"

"We're not coming," Henry said.

"It's all right, boy. I have a chicken, and we can get hamburger and bread and whisky in the village."

Henry told Emily to go and finish her coffee, but she refused. "You want to spoil the weekend, I can see it in your eye."

"Link," he said, "I'd rather not see any more of these people. There's something——"

Emily seized the phone. "Don't listen to him, Link. We'll be up. Henry's in one of his noble moods. He thinks we impose on you, but what are friends for? You'll love Miss Ada. I'll bring paper napkins. Good-by, dear." She snapped the phone before Henry could speak to Link again.

"That's fine," he growled. "We don't really know these characters, Emily. I'm not sure we want to."

"We'd better go find them," Emily said sweetly. "They must be through customs by now." She hurried Henry toward the stairs.

"I haven't any cash, and the banks are closed. You heard them say they have no American money and can't get any till Monday. Who's going to pay for the railroad tickets to Waterfall?"

Emily got over that one. They could take a cab. It would be cheaper in the end. Cheaper for whom? Henry muttered.

They found the little group and Emily told them her plan. Olivia thought it was a dreadful imposition, Miss Ada said they couldn't think of it, Mr. Peel said he wouldn't dream of exploiting them in this manner, and presently they were all in a cab.

"First we'll go to the studio to see if it's burned down or anything, and pick up the mail," Emily said. "And maybe we could get some roast-beef sandwiches from Mr. Gottlieb to eat on the way up to Link's."

"It will be cheaper in the end," Henry muttered.

They arrived at the studio, and the driver said he would wait and take them to Waterfall if they wished. Cabdrivers were usually interested in taking Emily places. She was better than radio.

"You can all come up and see what the place looks like if you want to," Emily offered, climbing out with her dressing case and shaking some of the wrinkles from her skirt.

Henry watched Miss Ada's face as she stepped into the Lentement Studio and cast an eye over the assorted frenzies of New York's best decorators. "It's like the attic in Marlborough." She sniffed. "What dreadful taste." She and Olivia walked down the narrow aisle to the back, exclaiming over tin pineapple sconces, iron nymphs on pedestals, workless wall clocks, tortured tables and chairs, padded headboards of Park Avenue beds, all awaiting Emily's paintbrush. When Henry had married Emily he had tried to bring system into the studio, but system and Emily were incompatible, and he now allowed things to take their natural course.

Roscoe had left a note pinned to the dangling light cord:

> *Mrs. E gonna kil yu*
> *Mrs. S tak bak sec*
> *Nobelly raze hell becuz yu go wa*
> *I tak pills evy day*
> *Male in desk*

"Poor Roscoe." Emily sighed. "He must have had an awful time. I knew we shouldn't go to London."

Mr. Peel said he hoped the trip hadn't damaged their business, and Henry assured him that these things went on all the time. "That commode in back of you has been half finished for eight months. The customer will have an apartment in purgatory before it's ready."

The phone rang. "How do they know we're back?" Emily wondered, taking it. "Hello, Alfredo. I don't know how you could have missed us. We were in the midst of the fray at the airport. You'd better hurry." She hung up. "What's he so steamed up about? He's coming over for the epaulets."

"I'm not waiting for Alfredo," Henry said. "He'll be all day getting here."

However, in eight minutes Alfredo Vittorio came panting up the stairs, his breath pushing with difficulty through his small bent nose. He had a soft pink face, tiny imbedded eyes, thin hair flattened to a large fat head, puffy hands, and a great deal of stomach balanced over a green leather belt. He was wearing lavender suede shoes, a maroon shirt, a cream-colored gabardine suit, and a couple of gold link bracelets.

He kissed Emily on the forehead. "Darling," he breathed. "I'm so glad you're back. And how is Mr. Murdock?"

He always referred to Henry by Emily's maiden name. Henry thought he did it on purpose, but Emily said he was just vague. Henry detested Vittorio.

"I'm spent," he went on in an exhausted, breathless little voice. "Absolutely spent. You don't know what this week has done to me, darlings. That bitch, Watkins, has been absolutely hounding me."

"Mrs. Watkins is not a bitch," Henry objected.

"I beg your pardon, she is one of the most mature, accomplished, and complete bitches of my entire acquaintance, and that includes a great deal of territory." Vittorio grinned suddenly. "Well, darlings, I want the present Jerome sent me. Where are the epaulets?"

Emily turned them over. "And this is Mr. Peel," she said. "He wants to tell you how much he liked the cabinets, don't you, Mr. Peel?"

Peel smiled, gingerly touched Vittorio's pink palm, and said the work was far beyond anything he had anticipated.

"Sometime we must have a talk," Vittorio said, smiling. "I want to hear all about my good friend Jerome."

Peel said that would be fine, but he looked as if he hoped it wouldn't happen.

Roy Palling, who had been lounging on a partly disemboweled settee, studied Vittorio as if he were some sort of bug. "I hear Jerome is making pots of money," he remarked. "Too rich to be honest."

"You know him?" Alfredo inquired eagerly.

"Only slightly."

Alfredo started to lower his rear into a chair but Emily arrested the movement. "You run along now, Vittorio," she said firmly. "Take your soldier's shoulders and go home. We're on our way up to the country for the weekend."

"Oh. Very nice. You're going to see your friend Simpson?"

Henry wished Emily would say no, because Vittorio had a habit of turning up for a meal. He owned a house somewhere in Putnam County, but people said he had never used the stove. Emily told him they were seeing Link. Vittorio said good-by, darling, to everyone, even Miss Ada, who turned her back, and departed with the epaulets.

"I'm glad he's gone, now I can call Mama," Emily said, picking up the phone. "Babylon 2262. Mama? We're back. Has anybody died or got married? We're going up to Waterfall to see Link. We brought back a couple of samples from London." Emily looked at Miss Birtwistle. "Human. No, only four. Link won't mind. Are you all right? Has anybody moved away? I know, but it seems like years, Mama." She hung up. "Well, let's go. What are we waiting for?"

"You," Henry said. "Why don't you leave those famous pants here and take the strain off your suitcase?"

Emily followed this suggestion, placing Charlie's pants in the drawer of a secretary. "They'll be safer here, anyway," she explained to Mr. Peel, in case he might think she didn't value the heirloom properly.

"I'm sure no one would take them," Mr. Peel agreed.

Henry looked around for burning cigarettes, took the mail, and they all went downstairs to the waiting taxi.

"The sandwiches!" Emily remembered. "Make mine roast beef."

Henry crossed the street to Gottlieb's Delicatessen and Restaurant, where Mr. Gottlieb was talking back to television and embroidering a tray of shrimp salad.

"Mr. Bryce," he cried, extending a muscular shrimpy hand. "You have a good trip? The missus enjoy herself?"

"Yes, we did, thanks. We're on our way up to the country to see Simpson. How about some roast-beef sandwiches and pickles and coffee and whatever else you've got that I can take out on credit. I'm strapped, Gottlieb."

"Your credit's good, Mr. Bryce. I put in some eclairs and a cheesecake? Your wife, she likes the sweets."

Henry shrugged. "How can she diet with you around, Gottlieb? Any news on the avenue?"

"Your friend in the beauty parlor is in some big oil deal. So I heard, anyhow."

"Hilda Leghorn in an oil deal?" Henry laughed. "I wouldn't want anything unpleasant to happen to Hilda, but I hope she put her life savings into a nice, comfortable swindle."

"She's nuts," Gottlieb agreed, "but she eats a lot. I gotta be nice to her."

"I see Mr. Vittorio finds you this morning," Gottlieb said as he put everything into a carton. "He went to your place every day, two, three times."

Henry grunted, took the carton, and returned to the taxi. He didn't have much time to think about Vittorio on the trip, between the mayonnaise and cheesecake Emily spilled on his sleeve and the questions Miss Birtwistle asked about the country, but he did wonder how Vittorio knew they would arrive this morning.

Going through Tarrytown, Miss Ada launched the race question. "What," she demanded, "is America doing to solve this problem?"

"Well," Henry answered, squirming slightly, "we're trying to educate people to be more reasonable."

"Useless, I should think," Miss Birtwistle dismissed the effort. "I've never known a reasonable human being in my life. Except myself, of course."

Henry noted that Mr. Peel wasn't listening to his cousin. He looked troubled, but perhaps this was only the uneasiness of a well-bred gentleman who finds himself forced to accept hospitality from strangers. Henry wondered how they would be able to put up with Roy at close quarters for a day and a half. If the weather held they could be out of doors most of the time, and then Link had a way of making things easier. People pulled in their quills when he talked with them.

It was four o'clock when they drove into Link's place. He came out of the garage with a hammer and a can of nails.

"Link, darling!" Emily cried, jumping out. "Put down the hammer, because they all shake hands when they're introduced."

Link made them welcome. He was very proud of the white cottage and the two acres of garden and lawn, bordered by a lusty mountain stream.

Roy, glancing toward the house, remarked pleasantly, "I'm afraid we're crowding you."

"No, not at all," Link assured him, not understanding Roy as yet. "We have four bedrooms."

"That's a comfort," Roy said. "Only seven of us."

Link, Henry could see, was beginning to get it. He smiled at Emily. "What did you tell them I had here, dear? Emily loves to build up her friends," he said to Roy. "But I'm just a junkman, and this was quite an achievement for me."

"Junkman!" Emily was indignant. "He's a notorious antique dealer." She walked over to the mound of luggage, picked out a brown-paper parcel tied with string, and handed it to Link. "I brought you a present, Link," she said gently. Henry was sure she had had no intention of giving him the silver coffeepot, but she wanted to make up for Roy, and this was her way of doing it. Oh well, they hadn't really needed it. Mr. Peel seemed to take the disposal of his present good-naturedly, and Link was delighted.

"I should like to see the gardens, Mr. Simpson," Miss Birtwistle suggested, throwing what charm she could over that gaunt frame, and resembling a suit of armor with lace pantaloons.

Link led the way through the paths around the rock garden and the azalea bushes and the vegetable plot and down to the little bridge that crossed the stream. "This runs into the swimming pool," he explained.

Henry was glad to see that the mention of a pool caught Roy off balance. It was curious that the ability to accumulate several gallons of water in a hole was so impressive to some people.

"I should like to see the swimming pool," Miss Ada stated.

The pool was at the back of the house and ran the full length of it. Doors opened onto the pool terrace from each of three bedrooms and from the porch off the living room. The pool was fed by the stream which ran all year, and at this time was roaring full and sent a heavy fall of water over the dam at the lower end.

Olivia bent down and put a hand into the water. "Chilly," she said.

"We don't generally use it till July," Link explained. "You swim, Mrs. Palling?"

"Not Olivia," Roy answered for her. "She's terrified."

"I don't care for it either," Link told her kindly.

Olivia thanked him with a smile, glanced at the bedroom doors along the terrace. "I should think one might fall into the water at night—if one were a sleepwalker," she said.

Roy gave her a curious look, as if something had just occurred to him. Henry didn't think it was anything pleasant, and he saw from Peel's face that he didn't think so either. Funny how they all seemed to be changing. Roy's obnoxious characteristics, which had been obscured somewhat by suave manners and easy circumstances, were sticking out like the bones on a hungry cow. Mr. Peel's urbanity was thinning—small lines of tension had formed around his mouth and between his eyebrows. He puffed differently on his pipe—in short, sharp jerks.

The only change in Miss Ada, however, was an alert interest in her surroundings. She wanted to drink in America in gulps, particularly the mechanical contrivances. When Link showed her the kitchen she stood a long time in front of the electric stove, snapping the buttons and watching the elements heat up. "If you like this one, you should see Andersons' up the road," Link told her. "It's like the engine room of a liner."

"Link," Emily called from the living room, "I wish you'd make up your mind about this house. Is it New England or is it Versailles?"

The former owners of the cottage had been strong for copper pots and rush-bottomed chairs, but Link leaned toward the Louis.

"I am not, thank God, a decorator," he reminded her. "I can do anything I please with my house." To prove it, he opened the window seat and took out a gilded sword, placed it on the stone mantel between a frying pan and a corn popper. "Genuine Toledo blade. Sharp too."

"All you need now is the Sheffield coffeepot and a coal shovel with a crocheted tassel," Henry suggested.

"Good idea," Link said, and he added the coffeepot to the collection.

What with showing the visitors the place and getting them located in bedrooms and counting out sheets and blankets and investigating the larder, it was dusk by the time Henry and Link started to town for groceries.

"What's the setup?" Link inquired. "There's something eating these people."

"You've noticed it?"

"How could I help it? They're all as jumpy as toads, except our friend Miss Ada. Where did Emily pick them up? Why are they here?"

"It was Peel who sent for Emily to do a pair of cabinets. That is, he sent for an American decorator, and Vittorio picked Emily. You've known Emily long enough to understand how the party grew to these proportions and who is going to pay for it. Although to be quite fair I don't think Emily suggested that they all come to the United States. There's some reason for their coming."

"They watch each other like tigers," Link remarked. "I'm glad I'll be sleeping in the garage."

They bought groceries and a case of beer. "Roy doesn't like beer," Henry explained. "May as well annoy him in small ways."

"I think we'll need whisky ourselves to get through a weekend with him. Why doesn't his wife cut his throat?"

"Olivia? Too well-bred."

"Those are the gals who pull the trigger, my friend. Nice, refined, repressed, inhibited people."

"Nuts. The English don't know when they're inhibited."

They started back to Link's place and had gone half a mile when Henry thought he saw a man walking toward them on the wrong side of the road. One rarely met people on foot.

"Any bad characters up here, Link?" he asked. "I think a fellow just took to the woods."

"I thought I saw someone," Link agreed. "They do have a robbery once in a while. Perfectly safe tonight, though, with all those people in the house."

When they turned into the drive Vittorio's opalescent convertible was at the door. Alfredo waved a limp hand from the kitchen step. "Greetings, kind friends," he murmured.

Link smiled because Link couldn't be unkind even to a nuisance like Alfredo.

"Don't be alarmed, will you?" Vittorio begged. "I shan't stay for dinner, even if you plead with me. I'm at the Andersons', up the road."

"Lucky for them," Henry grunted, pushing him aside with the box of groceries.

Olivia came from the living room with her father and they tried to help Henry and Link put away their purchases.

"I'm afraid we're a great deal of trouble," Olivia apologized.

"Think nothing of it." Link picked up two strange bottles from the table. "What's this? Madeira and scotch?"

Alfredo beamed all over; even his paunch seemed to glow. "I brought it, Simpson. For your English friends. I'm familiar with the tastes of the British. Haig and Haig for the gentlemen and madeira for the ladies."

"I detest scotch," Peel said promptly. "And Cousin Ada loathes madeira."

"Oh, but I adore madeira," Olivia put in quickly, smiling at poor Alfredo. She was like Simpson, couldn't bear to hurt people.

"Sweet lady," Alfredo breathed, taking up the bottle of wine, "I offer this humble gift to your exquisite beauty."

"Break it over his head," Henry suggested. "Launch him toward Andersons' so we can get dinner."

Peel liked that. He didn't care for Alfredo, and he looked relieved when the monstrous car crawled out the driveway. In fact, it seemed to Henry that Peel's animosity toward the decorator was almost too strong for so short an acquaintance.

"Where's Palling?" Link inquired. Olivia said he had gone for a walk.

"Didn't think he was the walking type," Henry remarked.

"There's something in the Magna Carta," Link explained. "If you're English you've got to walk."

Henry was at the sink adding water to a glass of whisky and ice cubes when Emily's face appeared at the window. She was wearing her urgent, mysterious look and wiggling a finger. Henry took the glass and went outside. Link followed.

"Matter? See a toad?" Henry asked.

"Shh." Emily led them to the far end of the garden, paused for effect, and announced, "Somebody has been through my luggage!"

"How could you tell?"

"Henry, this is serious. One of them was in our room looking for something."

"Probably looking for a bathroom," Link told her. "You know how it is in a strange house."

"If that's what they wanted, why did they dash out to the terrace and disappear when I opened the door?"

"Did you see this or just imagine it?" Henry wanted to know.

"There's a curtain on the door to the terrace and it was swinging, and somebody skinned around the house. I heard heels on the concrete."

Link groaned. "Too many *Official Detectives*. If we hear a scream in the night, it will be Emily having her throat cut again."

"Were the heels male or female?" Henry asked lightly.

"All right, have your fun. You'll see, you two." Emily turned away, remembered something. "Roy had a phone call, but I don't suppose you're interested."

"Roy?" Henry couldn't conceal his amazement. "Local or long-distance?"

"I don't know. He answered it himself."

"It wouldn't be any use asking you what he said because you don't listen to other people's phone calls."

"He said he'd call back. He wrote down a number."

"What was the number?"

"He didn't say it out loud, dopey. But I think it was a woman. Because he said it in a patronizing, putting-off sort of voice. At first he was mad. As if he hadn't expected to hear from this person."

Link said quickly, "Perhaps it was Roy who ducked into the woods as we came along the road from town."

Henry wanted to know where he would get the money to put in a phone call if he did go to town. Link said he left change lying around the house. Besides, there was Emily's handbag.

"That's what he was doing in our room!" Emily was indignant. "I've been robbed!"

"You wouldn't know whether you were robbed or not," Henry told her.

"But if he wanted money," Emily went on, "why didn't he take it from my bag? What was the point of going through my dressing case?"

"Did he?"

"Certainly he did. Everything's dumped out on the bed."

"You're sure it was Roy in our room?" Henry demanded.

"No. But it looks awfully suspicious for Roy, doesn't it?"

"Was Alfredo here when this happened?" Link asked.

"No, Roy went for a walk before Alfredo came."

"I don't know what you've imported, Emily," Henry said, disturbed, "but I don't think it's anything pleasant."

"I didn't make them come."

"You encouraged it."

"As soon as Roy said he was coming, then Mr. Peel said he was. And Miss Ada chimed in."

"Miss Ada is the only one who really liked the idea. But she didn't start it. Roy did. Who is watching who, that's what I'd like to know."

They were somewhat startled to see Miss Birtwistle coming across the little wooden bridge that crossed the brook.

"You ought not to wander about in the dark, Miss Ada," Henry said. "You might trip over a rock and break a leg."

"I know where to put my feet down. As a guest I ought not to mention it, but what is the customary hour for dinner?"

"Yes, what about it?" Emily chimed in. "I'm starved."

Link and Henry set to work—Emily couldn't be trusted with food—and they were sitting before the fire in the living room, finishing the first round of hamburgers, when Roy returned.

"Sorry I'm late," he said, perspiring. "I lost my way. Ought not to have gone out for the first time at night, I suppose. But I never can resist a walk."

Mr. Peel looked at him, didn't say a word.

Miss Ada, after two water glasses of sherry, declared herself in favor of the United States. "This was excellent," she said, "but what I look forward to most of all is the waffle. Shall we have that for breakfast, do you think?"

Link, who liked to please everyone, particularly old ladies, was disconcerted. "I don't have a waffle iron, Miss Ada," he said. "Perhaps we could borrow one."

"Maybe Miss Birtwistle would settle for flapjacks?" Henry suggested. "Very American too."

"Flapjacks would be very nice. I've read about flapjacks, I'm sure."

"I think if she wants waffles she should have waffles," Emily said decisively. "What's the matter with two able-bodied men who can't locate a waffle iron somewhere in Putnam County?"

Link thought perhaps the Andersons would have one—they had a power lawn mower and television.

"Cousin Ada didn't mean to put you to so much trouble," Olivia protested. "Really, it isn't that important, is it, dear?"

Miss Ada looked at her. "It is very important to me."

Roy yawned. "She's a pampered old thing, you know."

Link thought she ought to be pampered, and presently he and Henry took Miss Birtwistle and drove to the Anderson place about a mile up the road. As they came into the driveway Miss Ada inquired about the style of architecture.

"It's a Southern Colonial trunk with California ranch-house extremities," Link told her. "The garage is definitely Spanish, and I believe the tool shed is an authentic copy of Notre Dame. The furniture, naturally, is French provincial, with a dash of Crane, Kohler, and Westinghouse."

The inhabitants of this expensive bastard were an ingenuous middle-aged couple named Harry and Jane. They were delighted to lend a waffle iron and insisted on drinks all round. Miss Ada seemed to like them in spite of their bare thighs and worn tennis shoes. She did say it made her fidgety to see herself everywhere, but presently she forgot the Venetian-mirrored walls as she listened to Harry telling about the wholesale grocery business.

"Did you pass Vittorio on the road?" Jane asked abruptly.

Link shook his head.

"He drove into town. We sort of hoped he'd drop in on you for the night. He likes a crowd."

"Nice friends you are," Link grunted.

"He didn't say anything this morning about coming up to the

country," Henry observed. "It was through Vittorio that we went to London."

"Oh, really?" Jane leaned forward enthusiastically. "And did you have a marvelous time? How did you like the English? Oh, dear—" She cast an apologetic smile at Miss Ada.

"He's at liberty to make any statements he wishes," Miss Ada said. "As I shall do about your country. We are all most curious about your kitchens."

"Come and see ours," Jane offered eagerly. "We have everything."

Miss Ada followed, glanced unmoved at the yellow chintz curtains and the yellow trimmed cupboards and the pine walls, the deep-freeze, and the refrigerator. She made her way to the stove and studied the buttons. "One presses something and the heat is admitted?"

Jane pressed everything. Lights came on in the oven and at the back. "You set the clock and the alarm goes off when your cake is done."

"Marvelous," Miss Ada breathed. "I should spend all my time snapping these buttons."

"You like to cook, Miss Birtwistle?"

"Never cooked anything in my life." She returned to the living room. "Shall you be permanently cursed with these liver-colored walls?"

Harry laughed out loud. "Good for you, Miss Birtwistle. I've been fighting these walls alone for six months. Why can't people have nice cream-colored paint and ordinary paper like they used to have? Something you can look at without screaming?"

Miss Ada was studying the lighting fixtures above a grass-green sofa.

"They're just what you think they are," Harry assured her. "A taxidermist made them up. Took a week's profit from the sale of good sound cabbage and cheese to do it."

"Bats?" Miss Ada asked.

"Bats. Vittorio looked at us and he said, 'What will express the personalities of these people?' "

"I honestly don't care too much for the lighting," Jane admitted. "But when you hire a decorator you've got to let him use his own judgment, haven't you?"

"Ridiculous, I should say." Miss Ada helped herself to a cigarette and Harry lighted it. "I took an immediate and strong dislike to the man as soon as I encountered him."

The man in question came in at that moment, without knocking. "I can't say," she continued, looking straight at him, "that I have changed my opinion."

"Greetings, good people," Vittorio said with a sigh. "I could use a drink. I feel completely vitiated. But completely. One hasn't the strength to cope with this world."

Harry got up and poured. "Thought you were going to see some friends in the village?"

"I hadn't the energy somehow," Vittorio murmured, laying his limbs along the sofa and gently placing the back of his head on a pillow.

Link and Henry exchanged looks, and in a few minutes they had Miss Ada and the waffle iron in the car and were on their way back.

Emily had gone to bed. Mr. Peel and Roy sat before the fire with Olivia.

"I should think Vittorio would get tired of his own act." Link dropped into a chair and lighted a cigarette. "He's always just too, too weary."

"It struck me," Henry said, "that it wasn't an act this time. I really think something is bothering dear Alfredo."

Roy looked up, interested. Mr. Peel studied his watch chain and Olivia poured herself another little drop of madeira.

In a little while Henry said good night and went down the hall to the last bedroom on the right. There were three bedrooms on this side, the first assigned to Miss Ada, the second to Roy and Olivia, and the third to Henry and Emily. Each of these bedrooms had a glass door leading to the terrace around the pool. The porch off the living room also had a door which led onto this pool terrace. Mr. Peel's bedroom, across the hall from that occupied by Henry and Emily, was a sort of afterthought, making an el on that end of the house as the kitchen made one on the other end.

Emily was propped up in bed, churning through the *Daily News*. "How did Ada behave?" she inquired.

"Oh, very well. They liked her and we got the waffle iron. If Vittorio hadn't come in we'd probably still be there."

"Do you think he came over here for some purpose?" Emily
asked. "Alfredo doesn't give presents for nothing."

"He wants something," Henry agreed. He shed his clothes,
stretched on the good springs Link had provided.

"Do you like the sound of the waterfall, Henry?" Emily asked.
"I do. It reminds me of Niagara."

"You've never been to Niagara."

"I know. But it reminds me anyway. It's restful, like somebody
else pushing a lawn mower."

Miss Birtwistle piled the four pillows against the head of the cano-
pied bed, took out her teeth, put on her flannel bathrobe, and got
into bed. By great good luck there had been a copy of the *Deerslayer*
in the little bookcase over the desk. Fenimore Cooper was really
her favorite. Great pity no one could write like that nowadays. The
mattress was far too soft to be healthful. However, one had to admit it was comfortable. The whole room was comfortable, done in
pale greens, with nice old hunting prints on the walls, and odd bits
of china here and there, and plenty of ashtrays. She took a Virginia
cigarette from the package Henry had given her. Thoughtful person, that Henry. One could grow quite fond of these people. And
one felt a touch of remorse at having burdened them with Roy
Palling. They said everything in the universe, even the fly, had a
purpose. But of course Roy was born after these statements were
made. Poor dear Olivia, so stupidly defenseless. A prisoner of her
own feelings. She actually cared for Roy, no doubt about it. Quite
blind to his brutality.

Miss Birtwistle shrugged, pushed Roy from her mind, and turned
to Fenimore Cooper. But presently she was thinking of him again.
It would be easy to kill Roy during an Indian raid, but they didn't
have them any more—at least that's what the Americans claimed.
The arrows and shots flew thick and fast, and in the melee Roy
Palling ceased to breathe. Or one could drive him off a cliff with
the buffalo. Splendid splash at the bottom. He was sitting out there
by the fire, alone and quite stupid with whisky.

Olivia stood at the bedroom windows looking out on the rainy
night and listening to the roar of the water over the little dam at the

end of the pool. She thought about America, lying out there all around her, a vast, amazing country. If one could step outside and walk into America, all alone, free to go anywhere, to talk to anyone …

In a few days she would return to London with Roy. Everything would be just as it had been. Roy was not unreasonable. It was only that he wanted her to have more character. He was disappointed in her. She'd been pampered, he said, and it was true. Her father had always given her what she wanted. It was very wrong to do that with a child. One became soft and timid.

Roy deserved a better wife. Someone like Marie who could ride decently and was very strong and healthy and didn't have headaches and bad nights. Once she had mustered the courage to suggest a divorce, but Roy had appeared shocked.

"You're not serious, Olivia? Nice people don't have divorces. You must be thinking of the Americans."

Her father, too, had suggested a divorce to Roy, although he was terribly opposed to public disgraces of that kind. Roy said he was quite willing to put up with his bargain and saw no reason for any such drastic and scandalous action.

Now, looking out at the rain and the dark, she began to have alarming thoughts. "Why must I be like Marie?" she said aloud. "Why can't I be myself? I hate horses. I detest hunting and chasing poor animals. Why must I pretend not to? I loathe people when they've had too much to drink. Roy, sitting there all sodden and stupid. I hate Roy!" She found that her hand was crushing the linen drapery at the window.

She got into bed, very cold, and saw her own frightened face in the mirror on the opposite wall. "What is wrong with me?" she wondered. "Poor Roy has put up with such a lot, really."

She hunted feebly through the pile of old magazines on the lower shelf of the night table. "Perhaps he has put up with you for the sake of your father's money," she argued.

These doubts, she admitted, had not come suddenly out of nowhere. She recalled the evening when the Americans had arrived at the Royal Rajah. They were all sitting about the fire in the lounge and Roy had made a remark—she couldn't recall it now—but Emily had given him a look and said, quite audibly, "You big ape!" That had shocked Olivia, but it had given her a guilty pleasure too. Roy had defended himself against her father's criticism by saying, "Your father naturally doesn't care for me—no one would be good enough for our Olivia." And she had accepted that—her father was prejudiced. But here were two strange people who had no interest in "our Olivia" and they didn't like the way Roy spoke to her. That was the beginning.

"Olivia," she said, "stop thinking." And she bent her eyes fiercely on the page. But the words did not pass through her eyes. Roy was sitting out there by the fire, alone and quite senseless with whisky.

George Peel sat and looked at his son-in-law deep in a bottle, breathing heavily, his feet stretched toward the remains of the pleasant fire Mr. Simpson had provided earlier in the evening. He had ceased to wonder how Olivia could put up with the fellow. The fact was that she did put up with him. Too meek, too well brought up, Olivia. Sweet disposition, completely lacking in pride and backbone. If Roy said she was a coward about horses, she agreed with him and fell off again, just to confirm his judgment. Useless to hope she would ever see him as other people saw him, and take the necessary legal steps to get rid of him. Olivia would never divorce Roy.

Marie hadn't been good for Olivia. Nice enough girl, but she did everything too well. Made Olivia feel stupid and useless. Marie was never afraid. Marie charged about the world full of assurance and prune juice. Damn Marie, he thought. It was through Marie that Olivia had met Roy. Some hunt or other. Roy had immediately switched his attentions from Marie to Olivia, and there was no doubt in Mr. Peel's mind that the reason had been Olivia's money. Not that he didn't believe Olivia was beautiful and that a man might love her with or without money, but Roy liked money more than women. And he liked to torment people even more than he liked money. Marie hadn't appeared to resent Roy's decision in favor of Olivia. Hung around, still being friends. Or something like it, he added cynically.

What could a father do, anyway? Only hope that Palling would fall off a cliff or drink himself to death. One could administer judicious amounts of arsenic, but there were those annoying fellows, the police. Oh well. He sighed inwardly, knocked out his pipe, and said he would turn in.

Chapter 4

Henry was aware of a certain amount of tossing and groaning in the next bed. Emily probably had secretly finished the chocolate cake or opened a can of crab meat. He was accustomed to sleep with interference, so he pulled the sheet over his head and dozed off.

"I feel awful," Emily said loudly.

He heard, but he didn't move.

"Henry, please get me some bicarbonate."

Henry breathed evenly and didn't answer. After a minute or two Emily got out of her bed, worked her arms into her dressing gown, and staggered down the hall. She would drop a glass in the sink and fall over a couple of chairs, but there might be a few more hours of sleep if he didn't speak to her.

She came back rather quickly. In fact, she seemed to be running. He heard her knock into the telephone table in the hall, bang an elbow on the door frame, and then she stubbed a toe on his bed.

"What the devil are you doing, Emily? Can't you look where you're going?"

She made a funny gasping noise, and the bathroom door banged. Oh. Well, it was better to lose everything and make a fresh start.

He turned on the light and prepared to be sympathetic for five minutes. It was only half-past five.

The bathroom door opened and Emily said in a strangled whisper, "I can't get the blood off me, Henry."

Henry got out of bed. He looked Emily over and saw that her arm and her nightgown were smeared with a sticky maroon-colored substance. She was shaking all over.

"It's just paint," he said easily.

"It's blood. You can see it's blood. And there's somebody lying in it—I touched him when I slipped and fell."

Henry, still half-asleep, padded down the hall to the living-room doorway, flicked on the light.

A heavy man was lying in a dark puddle, his face pressed against Link's new green rug, his hands flung out as if he'd tried to break his fall. You could see that his throat had been opened up with something sharp. His shoes and socks were off and his pants pockets were turned inside out.

"It's Roy," Emily quavered, at his shoulder.

Henry stepped a little closer. He thought for a minute he might be going to make a quick trip to the bathroom himself, but then he became interested in the details and didn't feel sick any more. On the floor near the man's body lay the gilt sword, and standing on the hearth was the silver coffeepot. The sword was caked with dark stuff.

"That where you fell down?" he asked Emily, indicating a puddle that had been spread around on the rug.

Emily nodded. "Why is he in his bare feet? And what were they doing with the coffeepot?"

Henry didn't know.

"We can't just go back to bed and leave him here," Emily pointed out. "Aren't you going to call the police?"

"Naturally." Henry moved toward the phone on the hall table. "You run out to the garage and tell Link while I'm doing this."

"I will not. Do you want me decapitated in the rosebushes?"

"Oh, all right." The operator in Waterfall took a little time to wake up, but showed great enthusiasm when Henry asked for the police.

"Do you want the state police or the town constable?"

"I don't know. There's been a man killed at Simpson's place on the East Road."

"I'd better give you the troopers. Mr. Ballard wouldn't want to handle that, I'm sure."

Henry thanked her, and presently he talked to somebody in the state police barracks up the road. They'd be along.

"Why is everyone rising at this hour?" Miss Ada inquired from the doorway of her room, close to the telephone. Henry felt a little embarrassed at seeing her in a flannel nightgown, without her teeth.

He glanced involuntarily toward the living room. "It's nothing,

Miss Ada. Sorry to disturb you. Better go back to bed—that's what we're doing."

Miss Ada smiled tolerantly and stalked into the living room. Henry hoped she wouldn't faint or anything. She didn't even turn pale. "My, what a quantity of blood," she said.

"Aren't you surprised?" Emily demanded.

"Not particularly. Roy was the bleeding type. Odd that he should take off his shoes, isn't it?"

Mr. Peel's door opened at the end of the hall and he stuck out an inquiring face. "What's up?" he asked.

"Somebody's murdered Roy," his cousin answered cheerfully.

Mr. Peel came down the hall, obviously unwilling to believe her until he caught sight of the body on the floor. "I say," he muttered, going closer, his urbane face turned severe. "It's Roy. No doubt it's Roy. What do you make of it?" He turned to Henry, then seemed suddenly to remember Roy's connection with his daughter. "We've got to keep Olivia away. Terrible shock. No need for her to see him."

Miss Ada said she had to know sooner or later.

Olivia stopped the discussion by opening her door. "It's horribly early," she protested, looking sleepy and irritable.

"There's something you'll have to face, my dear," her father said gently. "I think you ought to sit down a moment."

"Oh, tell her the truth and let her sit down after she's heard it," Miss Ada said briskly. "Roy's dead, Olivia."

They watched Olivia. Henry thought she might be going to faint, but she blinked a few times and said, "I thought he looked ill last night."

"It was not an illness. His throat has been cut," Miss Birtwistle told her. "A very open sort of murder, no attempt to make it look like suicide."

Olivia put a hand on the doorknob to steady herself.

"Perhaps some whisky," Peel said to Henry, and Henry hurried to the kitchen, skirting the blood, came back with a bottle and a glass.

While they were busy with Olivia he ran out to the garage to wake Link. "Somebody killed Palling," he announced, "with your sword."

"What!" Link sat up. "Honest?" He leaped out of bed and into his trousers. "Did you call the troopers?"

"Yes."

"Everybody else up? How'd Olivia take it?"

"Very well. Surprisingly well, in fact. Wonderful control."

"I'd have said she was the fainting type," Link muttered, buttoning the middle button of his shirt and squeezing his feet into loafers.

"So would I. But she isn't." They went into the house together.

"Miss Ada and I found something," Emily cried, not giving Link time to take in the scene. "Globs of blood from Roy to the swimming pool—through the porch and out to the terrace. I don't see how he could take a walk with his throat cut, do you?"

"You're not supposed to tramp around in the evidence," Henry said sternly. "Where's the blood?"

They showed him the drops, close together near the body, and spaced at longer and longer intervals as the distance from the body increased.

Link circled the terrace, throwing his flashlight into the pool, but he couldn't see anything. The water was cloudy in the spring when the stream tore along taking dirt and leaves with it, and the raindrops hitting the surface completed the opacity.

"One might conclude that something had been thrown into the pool," Miss Ada remarked, standing on the edge and looking in, a majestic if somewhat surprising figure in a brown bathrobe with a long, heavy cord, Turkish slippers, and a wool stocking cap.

Henry heard Olivia whisper to her father as they hung in the background, "I do wish Cousin Ada would dress."

Link said he would make coffee. It was still too early to consider breakfast. They all followed him to the kitchen, no one seeming anxious to be alone. The house had shadowy corners although every light was on. Link asked Olivia to reach into the cupboard behind her and take down some heavy china mugs, and Olivia, seeming glad of something to do, made a great thing of it. There was a bit of dust in the mugs, she said, and Henry handed her a dish towel from the rod near the sink. Suddenly she let go of both the towel and the mug. She stood looking at the mess of broken china and the little heap of linen at her feet.

"I'm terribly sorry," she stammered. "I thought it was—blood. On the towel."

Link picked it up. "Anybody's apt to be jumpy at a time like this, Mrs. Palling. Don't think a thing about it. You see it's perfectly—" He held the towel up to the light. "My God, the lady's right."

Henry saw a look of satisfaction cross Miss Ada's somewhat dehydrated face. The finding of blood on a dish towel, he thought, was a rather unusual source of pleasure. But then Miss Ada was a highly unusual gal.

Link placed the towel carefully on a shelf, for police reference, brushed the fragments of china into a dustpan, and poured the coffee.

It seemed to Henry that the dish towel had a very unnerving effect—it gave them all a feeling of being surrounded by stealthy violence, a fear that any homely thing they touched might also have been touched and used by the murderer. At first the horror had been localized, confined to the area around the body, so that you felt comparatively safe in any other room. Now it had been demonstrated as occupying an unknown area.

"Emily left a pan, as usual," Henry remarked lightly, trying to ease things. "Never washes everything."

"I did not leave a pan. I actually scoured out the sink and polished the faucets. Olivia and Link will tell you—they were here."

"Oh yes? What's this, then? Looks like milk sticking to the bottom of it." He held up the aluminum saucepan for them to see. There was a glass, too, with a trace of milk in it.

Link thought someone had heated milk before going to bed. No one admitted having done so.

"Perhaps Roy did," Miss Ada suggested. "Although from my experience I should say he was much too lazy to heat a glass of milk."

"He was too far gone when I left him to have bothered," Mr. Peel said. "I don't believe it was Roy."

"The murderer?" Emily suggested.

"Very casual fellow, if he did," Link remarked, blowing on the hot coffee. "Where's the law? Seems to me they're a long time coming."

Henry went outside to have a look up the road, and Miss Ada

followed him. It was growing light now. Color hadn't come into the flowers and the lawn, but the shapes of things were clear.

"What do you make of this, Mr. Bryce?" Miss Birtwistle asked abruptly.

"Looks like a nice, intimate family murder to me."

"You don't think one of us killed Roy?" Miss Ada put on a shocked expression.

"Since he's just arrived in this country no one here would have any reason to murder him, Miss Birtwistle."

"But you do have an unreasonable murder now and then, don't you? Gangsters and the insane and millionaires?"

Henry admitted that not all killing was rational in his country. "But Roy was not a welcome member of the family, was he?" he persisted. "You and Mr. Peel rather pitied Olivia, didn't you? And I shouldn't be surprised if she pitied herself."

"Oh, nonsense. If she liked she could have had a divorce."

"But she preferred to be pitiable."

Miss Ada sniffed. "Olivia is not like that at all. She has a lamentable strain of illusion and romantic claptrap. Her mother was Irish, you know. The Irish always find the undersides of things more interesting than the tops. There's no helping them, because they don't wish to be helped. No one is more at loose ends than an Irish person without a sorrow."

"And Roy was Olivia's sorrow?"

Miss Ada didn't like that, either. "I believe she liked being married to Roy."

"She was afraid of him."

"Then she enjoyed being afraid of him. Are you going to say all these dreadful things to the police, Mr. Bryce?"

"Certainly not. Let the police do their own work."

They were standing beside the pansy bed, and Miss Ada suddenly bent down. "Footprints!" she exclaimed. "There, I knew it was a gangster."

There were indeed fresh footprints in the wet spaded earth. They led from the graveled drive to within a few inches of the living-room windows, and had apparently been made by a man's shoes, although Miss Ada's stout walkers could have made similar impressions.

At that moment a motorcycle roared down the hill and into the drive, spitting gravel.

"Trouble here?" the trooper demanded. He was a good-looking blond young man with tired circles under his eyes.

They took him inside, and after a brief look at the body he asked where the phone was and put in a call for assistance. Then he asked a great many questions.

"Young man," Miss Birtwistle finally said, with ice in her voice, "if you had been through the London raids you would not make so much of one dead man."

For the first time the fellow smiled. He was rather likable, Henry decided, and being severe only because he felt a little young. His name was Conlan and he hadn't been getting much sleep, he said, because his wife had recently acquired two chow puppies who cried all night.

"You wouldn't mind sitting up with a baby," he explained, "but a couple of pups—it makes you sore."

Emily said they would have to get a nurse for them, or a mother dog. "Why don't we have a dog, Henry?" she demanded. "If we'd had a dog here last night nothing like this could have happened."

"I don't see how it happened anyway," Conlan said, "without one of you hearing a noise."

Link took him by the arm. "I'll explain that." He led Conlan through the porch to the terrace beside the pool. "Hear that waterfall? That noise in the bedrooms is loud enough to drown anything else."

"Anyway," Emily put in, "how much noise does a man make when his throat is cut?"

"No one heard a car drive into the place?" Conlan went on, making notes in his book. No one had. Link explained that he had slept in the garage and would surely have heard any car that came down the driveway from the road.

"But they would leave the car some distance away," Miss Ada objected. "No one would be fool enough to drive up to the house if he intended committing a murder."

The experts began to arrive. First came the medical examiner, then a photographer and a technical man, and finally a more mature officer, Sergeant Myron Fisher. Fisher had a slow, easy voice but his eyes were very busy.

Emily and Miss Ada watched the men unload their equipment. "I hope you're going to make a *moulage*," Emily said. "I've never seen anybody make a moulage."

"What of?" Fisher inquired. "Any footprints, Conlan?"

Miss Ada and Henry said nothing, and Conlan flushed. He hadn't looked. It seemed to him, he said, like an inside job.

"Rather early to decide that," Fisher murmured. "Doors locked?"

"No," Link told him. "I was sleeping in the garage. It didn't seem necessary to lock the house."

Fisher asked to see the bedrooms, and Emily suffered a horrible indecision. She wanted to hear what Fisher had to say and she wanted to see the men working in the living room.

She finally went with Fisher, and Henry and Miss Ada stayed to watch the activity around Palling's body. As soon as the photographer had finished, the other fellow got to work, taking samples of blood from the carpet, the chair arm, the sword, and the spatterings that led to the terrace. He dusted powder here and there with his little feather duster and found a few prints that showed up well, including one on the outside kitchen doorknob.

They sketched the room, collected cigarette ends, dust, and lint. They fingerprinted everyone in the house. They tied the sword to a board and put it into one of the cars. Finally the medical examiner removed the body.

"I'm glad to have him out of the way," Miss Ada remarked, watching Roy's bare feet disappear into the car. "One can be more objective about a murder once the corpse has been disposed of. Did you notice, Mr. Bryce, that there was only one shoe?"

Henry hadn't noticed. The old girl was right on the job. Conlan came in to report the footprints in the flower bed under the living-room windows, and Fisher, having completed his survey of the bedrooms, went outside to look.

"There is no door directly into the living room," Fisher said aloud. "You enter from the hall or from the kitchen. But first you'd like to see who's in there. So you look through these windows. Mr. Palling is sitting alone in front of the fire. So you step out of the flower bed and open the kitchen door."

"They took a good print from the doorknob," Conlan told him.

Henry pointed out that several people had gone through that door since the body had been discovered. Fisher was still looking at the footprints. They led to the window, and then came back to the drive at almost the same angle.

Of course you couldn't be sure, but it seemed to Henry that the man had been alarmed by what he saw and had retreated rapidly. Otherwise, Henry reasoned, he would have gone toward the kitchen door rather than back again.

To Emily's delight they made a moulage, while Fisher constructed a picture of the guests in the house. Henry, Emily, and Link were cautious in their replies to his questions, and Roy's relatives were extremely noncommittal, but Fisher remarked presently, "So he was a first-class heel, eh?"

"Oh yes," Emily said, relieved. "We didn't want to say so, but since you've found it out, he really was a stinker. Nobody wanted him around—he was spoiling the whole weekend."

"Was there a certain amount of tension even before you left Britain?" Fisher asked Henry.

"No more than in any family where one member is objectionable," he said, embarrassed. Olivia was watching him.

"You tell me, Mrs. Bryce, that you were hired by a decorator to go to London to paint some furniture. Was there no one in England who could do this work?"

"Oh, I imagine there must be people," Emily said modestly.

Link spoke up. "She's the best in her line—no one can touch her."

"Oh, Link," Emily protested. "There are other people who can do what I do. I learned from an Italian."

"But he's dead," Link reminded her.

"You really ought to question me," Peel said reasonably. "I employed Mrs. Bryce to do this work."

"Was it your idea?"

"No, I'm afraid not. A London decorator suggested it. Jerome. Perhaps you've heard of him?"

Fisher shook his head. "Don't know beans about the business. First time I ever heard that they swapped painters across the Atlantic. Big job?"

"Two cabinets. Not a big job," Henry put in.

Link said he didn't see why the sergeant was making so much of the fact that Emily had gone to London to do a bit of antiquing. "They exchange people all the time," he said.

Fisher smiled. "I merely want to have things clear in my own mind. It's common, then I take it, for a decorator in London to hire a painter from New York and pay his way over for a two- or three-day job?"

"Not common," Henry put in. "But it's done. It amuses them to be international, shall we say?"

"An imported flyspeck is a more distinguished flyspeck," Emily said. "Do you want to see what I do?" She took the sergeant's arm and led him to the porch. "I marbleized this table. Doesn't it look real?"

"Positively cold," Fisher admitted.

"We could use it in the morgue." Conlan touched it admiringly. "It must be quite a trick to do that."

"Oh, it's nothing," Emily said.

"Now, to get back to the murder," Fisher went on, turning to Mr. Peel. "When did you people decide to come to the United States?"

Peel cleared his throat, flushed slightly. "I had no such plans, to be quite truthful, until my son-in-law announced his intention of making the trip."

"You came along to be with him?"

"No. To be with my daughter. She has not been very well."

Fisher turned to Olivia, whose policy during the inquisition was to be as quiet and insignificant as possible. "Mrs. Palling," he said gently, "you could go and lie down if you wish. No need to stay around. I can talk to you tomorrow just as well."

Olivia gave him her fragile smile, but Fisher didn't appear to notice it. Wary of feminine charm, probably. "I'm not ill, Sergeant," she said. "Really I'm not."

"You may not realize it yet, but you've had a severe shock. Better lie down."

"I feel safer with all of you."

"Just as you say," Fisher agreed. "But I don't think you need worry about further violence. These things don't come in bunches, you know."

Miss Ada spoke up. "I was under the impression that they did, in America."

"You're thinking of gang warfare, Miss Birtwistle," Link told her. "This is a private affair."

"How do you know, Mr. Simpson?"

"I'm sure Mr. Palling hadn't time to get mixed up with a gang in one afternoon."

"Perhaps," Miss Ada persisted, "he was already mixed up in one."

Henry helped her, just to keep the argument going. "Roy did go to town. And on a secret mission, apparently, because he ducked into the woods when we came along."

Fisher was interested. He asked questions, and Emily told him about Roy's telephone conversation. He put Conlan to work tracing the call. "Find out what Palling did while he was in town," he ordered. "He may have made several phone calls. Did your husband know people in this country?" he asked Olivia.

"I'm sure he didn't. We were very glad to be asked to come here for the weekend until we could get to the bank on Monday."

"So this party was a sort of financial convenience, eh?" Fisher suggested.

Mr. Peel objected to that, but Miss Ada said honestly, "We were all four quite stony, George, and you know it."

"Why did you come along, Miss Birtwistle?" Fisher asked her abruptly.

"I?" She measured him. "I came for the ride. I've never been in a plane before."

The sergeant's eyebrows indicated a certain skepticism, but he didn't press Miss Birtwistle. "No previous acquaintance with these people, Bryce?" he asked. Henry said no, none.

"Do you mind if I ask some rather impertinent questions?" Fisher looked from Olivia to Miss Ada to Mr. Peel.

"Not at all," Miss Ada said agreeably. "Should I be considered callous if I suggested that we have the waffles, as we planned?"

"Good idea, Miss Ada," Link said. "I'm hungry. Maybe the sergeant will have some too?"

Fisher said he was very fond of waffles and he could use a cup of strong coffee. He sat down at one end of the marbleized table and was busy with a pencil and his own thoughts for some minutes while Link turned out waffles and Henry poured glasses of canned orange juice and laid paper napkins under forks to keep them from blowing away. Conlan was still at the phone in the hall. The technical men finished their work and drove off.

When everyone was seated except Link, Fisher took up his inquiry again. He asked Peel about his finances, and Peel said he had sold his interest in the chemical business and retired. He had also sold his country place and planned to live in London to be near Olivia.

"This furniture Mrs. Bryce was painting," Fisher inquired, "was it for you, Mr. Peel?"

"No. For my daughter and her—late husband. They took a flat in Mayfair and I was helping them furnish it."

"Was this help necessary? Was Palling dependent on you?"

"No indeed, Sergeant," Olivia said sharply. She looked at her father as if to prevent his making a contradictory statement. "Roy was a reputable barrister and quite independent of my father."

"You agree with that, Peel?"

"Umm. Yes."

"Your efforts were the natural inclination of a doting parent to make life more luxurious for your daughter?"

Peel nodded.

"Did Palling resent your interference?"

"There was no interference," Peel told him firmly.

"Your chemical business was a substantial affair?"

"It was a fair business." Peel said this modestly, but Henry got the impression that it had been a very good business.

"What made you retire? You appear to be a healthy, energetic sort of man."

"I've never believed in driving oneself up to the last moment of one's life. Why not take one's leisure before it's too late to enjoy a good bottle of whisky or a walk in the country or—a plane ride to America?" He smiled.

Conlan came in. "I've got some phone numbers. Someone called this number twice, once from the house here and once from town. The operator thinks it was a man. He also called this other number from town." He handed Fisher a slip, and Emily leaned over and looked at it.

"Didn't you try to find out whose numbers they are?" Fisher demanded.

"Yes, sir. They're working on it." He went back to the phone.

"Plaza 3-7918," Emily read aloud. "Henry, doesn't that ring a bell?"

"No," Henry said. "And the sergeant would appreciate it if you wouldn't look at his hand."

"Then he'd better hold his cards against his chest," Emily replied. "That's Vittorio's number."

Fisher wanted to know who Vittorio was, and they told him. They also told him that Vittorio had planned to spend last night with the Andersons up the road.

"He must have been there when Roy called him in New York," Link said.

"I thought you said Mr. Palling didn't know anyone in the United States before he came here?" Fisher snapped.

"He met Vittorio yesterday in the studio," Emily explained.

Fisher made another notation and looked puzzled. "You're quite sure Palling had no connection with this Vittorio before he met him yesterday?"

Mr. Peel looked at his daughter. "As far as I know he had none. Roy of course knew Jerome. We all saw Jerome frequently while he was doing the flat for my daughter."

"Has there been anything unusual about Palling's behavior during the last few days?"

"Only this walk to town," Olivia said. "My husband was not fond of walking."

"Obviously wanted privacy for his phone calls."

"There was something else," Emily admitted. "I think it was Roy who went through my dressing case."

"Really!" Olivia protested, shocked.

"When Henry and Link were gone. I didn't actually see him, but I had the idea it was somebody pretty bulky," Emily continued. "He hotfooted out to the terrace when I opened our door."

Fisher appeared to find this interesting, but he made no comment.

Link brought Miss Ada a waffle, and she began tucking it away with evident pleasure. It was doubtful if she considered Palling's sudden end half so important as her first waffle. She was a tough old bird, Henry reflected, one of the last of a generation with steel nerves and iron prejudices.

Conlan returned with more information from the phone company. The second number, called from the village, was that of the Hotel Lexington in New York. Whether Roy had spoken to someone there they didn't know. All the operator had done was connect him with the hotel switchboard. Fisher sent Conlan back to talk with the desk at the Hotel Lexington, but that call was fruitless.

"Get in touch with the Seventeenth Precinct and ask them for a transcript of the hotel register for the last four days," Fisher ordered. He turned to Mr. Peel and Olivia. "When we get that I hope you'll tell me if you recognize any of the names. The difficulty is, of course, that the person Mr. Palling called may have registered under a false name."

"Or he may be someone we do not know," Olivia added.

Fisher questioned Link, but they were able to convince him that Simpson was the innocent victim of Emily's hospitable impulses.

"I've got to drain your pool, Simpson," the sergeant announced. "We'll try to do as little damage as possible to your place. I'll send some men over this afternoon. Can't see any reason for the murderer to come out to the terrace—which he must have done to leave those drops of blood—unless he threw something into the pool."

Link tried not to show the concern he must feel for his property. Miss Ada and Emily appeared pleased. Any activity was duck soup to them.

"That about does it for now," Fisher concluded, capping his ballpoint pen and buttoning his coat. "I expect you all to remain here today. We'll talk about tomorrow later."

"What are you going to do now, young man?" Miss Ada inquired.

Fisher didn't seem to mind her curiosity. "I'm going to see Mr. Vittorio."

A visit from an officer of the law, Henry reflected, would probably give Vittorio a stroke. He was overcome by the sight of the wrong shade of pink.

Conlan and Fisher left. There was silence for a moment, and then Emily, looking round the table, remarked, "Wouldn't it be funny if somebody here killed Roy?"

Undoubtedly everyone had been considering this possibility, but only Emily would come out with it.

Link smiled. "If one of us did, I'm sure he had a good reason."

"I should not have done it that way," Miss Ada said scornfully. "I should have dealt him a blow with one of those logs and then burned the log. No murder weapon. Very confusing."

Mr. Peel smiled. "As a chemist I find your suggestion crude, Cousin Ada. There are ways of killing a man chemically, leaving few if any clues. It seems to me this crime was done in sudden anger, or by someone with no imagination."

"You'd think Palling would have tried to defend himself," Link observed. "It looked as if he just fell over like a ton of bricks, no alarm, no clutching or fighting."

"He was well on his way to an alcoholic stupor when I went to bed," his father-in-law explained. "He may have been asleep when the attack was made."

It did look as though he had dozed in his chair in the living room. The doors were unlocked. He had sat facing the windows toward the driveway, his helpless condition plainly visible to anyone who might have pressed a curious face to the glass.

"He could not possibly have killed himself, I suppose?" Olivia asked timidly.

Her father raised a quizzical eyebrow. "Nobody seems to think so, my dear. It would have been considerate of Roy to kill himself, but I doubt very much if the thought ever crossed his mind. I have been wondering why the Sheffield coffeepot was on the floor."

"So have I," Link admitted. "I don't see what connection it could possibly have had with the killing. Perhaps it was knocked off when the murderer took the sword from the mantel."

Emily went into the living room and took down the coffeepot. "It hasn't a single dent anywhere," she said. "And it was lying on the stone hearth."

Henry corrected her. It had been standing on its legs on the hearth.

"The chances of its falling that way from the mantel would be pretty slim, I should think," he remarked. "Someone set it there, carefully."

"Roy?" Emily demanded.

"If it was Roy, he was engaged in some funny games with himself. First he took off his shoes and socks, then he set a silver pot on the hearth, then he tossed everything out of his pockets onto the floor."

"And where is Roy's other shoe?" Miss Ada asked.

They batted these questions around for a while, and then Henry announced that he was going for a walk.

"A walk!" Emily cried. "In the middle of a murder?"

"Very bracing, a walk," Miss Ada informed her, but she took out her knitting and did not offer to be braced.

"Would you mind very much if I went with you?" Olivia asked.

"Not at all." Henry was pleased. "Better wrap up well; it's chilly."

They found an old raincoat and a windbreaker of Link's, some assorted fishing hats, and a pair of rubbers for Olivia.

Emily regarded these preparations with open suspicion, but she didn't say anything. Making up her mind what line to take, Henry thought as he said good-by and followed Olivia outside. There was a fine, cold rain blowing, wetter than a downpour.

"I should think you'd want to rest, Mrs. Palling," Henry said as they reached the road at the top of the drive and turned left. "Cigarette?"

"Thank you." She took it gratefully, her fingers trembling slightly. "Walking is restful. I like the rain and the odor of the woods."

Chapter 5

Henry let Olivia set the pace. It was a little brisk for his well-rested muscles, but he tried to puff inaudibly. The fragile Olivia was tougher than she looked. It occurred to Henry, studying the sweep of eyelash on the creamy skin, that she had come with him to escape observation by her two overanxious relatives.

"Do you suppose this would have happened had Roy remained in London?" she asked matter-of-factly.

"Only one person can answer that," Henry pointed out.

"Have you anyone in mind?"

"Have you?" he countered.

"I keep wondering why Roy called your Mr. Vittorio. I'm almost certain he didn't know Mr. Vittorio. In fact, he had very little to do with Jerome. My father consulted with Jerome, made all the arrangements. Roy was bored with the flat, really."

Henry said perhaps the footprints in the flower bed had been made by Vittorio.

"Looking in the window to make sure Roy was there alone?"

"If he came to see Roy."

"Who else would he have come to see?"

Henry shrugged. It was possible that Vittorio wanted to talk with Mr. Peel, or with Olivia herself. Perhaps even Miss Birtwistle. For who had less reason to come to America than Miss Ada, when you thought about that?

They were walking along the highway, but very few cars passed them. The weather was keeping the weekend traffic at a minimum. Rain glistened on the hazel bushes and rolled off the violets and some striped pink flowers blooming in little clumps in the grass at the side of the road. They were going in the direction of Andersons', for Henry had it in the back of his mind to stop there and see what effect Fisher's call had had upon Vittorio.

"Tired?" he asked.

"Oh no." She put on more speed, and Henry was sorry he had spoken.

When they came within sight of the Anderson house there were no vehicles indicative of a police visit. He told Olivia that this was where Vittorio was staying and asked if she would mind going in for a minute.

"Not if you don't tell them who I am. It would seem odd, I'm sure, for the widow to be out calling." She smiled a little, and they trudged down the blue gravel drive.

Jane and Harry both came to the door. "Henry, come on in!" Harry cried. "We've got dirt to spill."

"The police were here," Jane told him, "and who do you think they were looking for? And he wasn't here because he picked up his tents and vanished during the night. What do you know?"

"Who vanished?" Henry grinned, dropping into one of their bottomless armchairs and helping himself to one of their Virginia Rounds. They didn't seem to notice Olivia who had taken a chair near the fire and was looking around.

"Vittorio, of course," Harry said. "What do you suppose our dear Alfredo has been up to? Dirty work of some kind, that's sure. We gave the cops his New York address."

"They won't find him there," Jane interrupted. "He's scared out of his wits or he wouldn't have gone before breakfast. Who is the lady, Henry? Your manners are awful."

"Give me a chance. Olivia, these chattering idiots are Jane and Harry Anderson. You wouldn't have a drink for a couple of lost souls, would you, Harry?"

Harry jumped up, always delighted to pour. "How did Miss Birtwistle like the waffles?" he wanted to know.

"Very much. She's sold on America, isn't she, Olivia?"

"Rather."

"You're English too," Jane pounced.

"She's pure Long Island," Henry lied, not wanting them to question Olivia. "What did the police have to say about Vittorio?"

Jane indignantly gave her opinion of the tight-lipped Sergeant Fisher who had told them exactly nothing. "We've got private sources in Waterfall, though. Harry talked to the telephone girl and she says there's been a murder up here. As soon as she finds out where she's going to call us back. That's the kind of telephone service I like, don't you, Henry?"

"Excellent. Let me know when you hear the news."

"Funny they should want Alfredo in connection with a murder," Harry murmured, tasting his own drink with appreciation. "He's afraid of a rare steak."

"You don't know when he left last night, I suppose?"

"No. We were asleep," Jane told him. "When we found his bed empty and the car gone we were sure he'd only dashed into town for the papers and would be back. On a day like this I'd welcome almost any company, even Vittorio."

"Not me," Harry grunted. "If I never see that doughy face again it will be okay with me. How about a fast game of poker, you two?"

Henry thanked him, said they must get back. As they walked up the drive he had a feeling that Olivia would have liked to stay.

"They are amusing, aren't they?" She looked back at the house somewhat wistfully. "You don't understand how amazing it is to find oneself in America. Do you know that for a moment I almost forgot Roy?"

"It was worthwhile coming, then," Henry said. "I'd have asked them over, only it didn't seem quite the thing."

Olivia agreed that it wasn't quite the thing, and they walked on in silence, Henry busily wondering what Vittorio could have had to do with anything so violent as Palling's exit from this world.

When they reached Link's place Henry suggested cutting down the bank and through the rock garden instead of going round by the driveway. His feet hurt. He turned his ankle, caught himself with the aid of an azalea bush, sat down in the mud.

"Oh, dear," Olivia cried. "Are you hurt?"

"Mortally." He started to get up, noticed something white under the bush. It was a cigarette stub, the paper opened by the rain and almost covered with tobacco. He picked it up. Virginia Round. "Alfredo was here last night," he said aloud. "He never smokes his own cigarettes."

Olivia looked about. "If there were any footprints we've ruined them."

Henry didn't think there had been any, or Fisher and his men would have found them. They had done a thorough job. "Vittorio probably tossed that up here as he walked along the driveway. No one found it this morning because the paper was practically covered."

They went into the house where Miss Ada was still knitting in front of the fire. Link and Mr. Peel had joined her, and everyone looked up with relief at the sight of Henry and Olivia.

"We dropped in at Andersons'. It seems that Alfredo fled during the night. It also looks as if he'd been here." Henry showed them the cigarette paper. "Harry Anderson's brand. Found it in the rock garden. Where's Emily?"

"She made herself a roquefort-and-ketchup sandwich," Link reported, "and went back to bed to think. What makes you so sure Vittorio didn't drop that cigarette when he came here before supper with the liquor?"

"Too far from the driveway to be flipped out of a car, and he wasn't walking around, was he, Olivia?"

"No," she said definitely. "He stayed here in the house."

Henry went back to their room and found Emily behind a ladies' magazine.

"I've been expecting it," she said.

"What?"

"The breakup of our marriage. But I always thought it would be Mrs. Cormorant. All that money, and she isn't really bad-looking except for a hooked nose and glasses and little eyes and bumpy skin."

"What are you talking about?" Henry slid off his wet shoes and socks.

"You and Olivia."

"I'm not interested in Olivia."

"Well, why aren't you? Something ought to happen to our marriage. According to Dr. Samson Bertolini, marriages go on the rocks during the third or the tenth year."

"Let's wait till the tenth year," Henry suggested amiably. "Who is Dr. Samson Bertolini?"

"He's a very famous man, anybody knows that."

"What's he a doctor of?"

"Just because you're ignorant and haven't heard of him, you have to be superficial."

"I just asked what he's a doctor of."

"The *Ladies' Home Journal*——"

"Doctor of the *Ladies' Home Journal*. We found one of Vittorio's cigarettes in the rock garden."

"You and Olivia?"

"What is this business? You were never jealous before."

"I know. I've been very lax."

"Why do these female magazines always harp on the husband? Haven't women got anything to think about but their husbands?"

"Was it really Vittorio's cigarette, Henry?" Emily asked, suddenly becoming normal. "How do you know?"

He told her why he thought so, and added that Vittorio was missing. Emily knew immediately where he was. "Remember, Henry, he has a place near Fishkill. Not in his own name—Mrs. Cormorant told me that. He's always afraid of being sued, so it's in his sister's name. He's hiding out there. Henry, what about my shoes? That was the first suspicious thing that happened, taking the heels off my shoes in the Royal Rajah. You know the porter didn't do that."

"I don't suppose he did."

"People smuggle dope in their shoes."

"Do they?" Henry asked. "I've never met anyone who did."

"You know they do. And remember the way the package was returned? If the porter had found that package he'd have knocked at the door and handed it to us instead of leaving it on the floor outside."

Henry said perhaps she was right, but he couldn't picture a dope ring operating around the highly respectable Mr. Peel. "Or was it Miss Ada you had in mind?"

"I'm thinking of Roy." Her eyes opened very wide. "Henry, do you suppose Roy was going to make me smuggle dope in my shoes and then get it away from me when we reached the United States?"

"Of course," Henry grunted. "Nothing could be more obvious."

"And Vittorio was in it," she continued, enjoying the idea. "But Roy double-crossed him, so he had to wipe Roy out."

"Vittorio couldn't wipe out a gravy spot. And you seem to forget that there was nothing in the heels of your shoes."

Emily said that was simple—they'd decided to put the dope somewhere else. "Henry, that's what Roy was looking for in my dressing case!" She leaped out of bed, seized the case and dumped its contents on the sheet. "What does dope look like?"

"Depends on the kind, I think. White powder, maybe. I don't know."

"Tooth powder, Henry. That would be the easiest place to hide dope, wouldn't it? I've felt funny ever since I brushed my teeth."

Henry grinned, but he did unscrew the top of the box and sniff the contents. "I wouldn't know it even if this were loaded with opium. Smells like peppermint to me. And if Roy had put the stuff in here, he'd have been able to snatch it instantly, instead of rummaging through all your belongings."

Emily agreed, though he could see she hated to let go the idea that she had brushed her teeth with opium. She continued to paw through her underwear, jewelry, Kleenex, and assorted trash.

Link and Miss Ada came to the door. "Miss Ada wants to play poker," Link said.

"One has to do something," Miss Ada explained. "I detest knitting."

Mr. Peel came along. "She's been working on that same sock since the Boer War."

"Come in and sit down, everybody," Emily invited. "I'm looking for dope."

"Emily has a new theory that Roy planted valuable drugs in her paraphernalia. Vittorio killed Roy because he wouldn't split. Isn't that interesting?" Henry grinned.

"What brought this on?" Link wanted to know.

Henry related the incident in the Royal Rajah, and Link said maybe the porter was going into the shoe-repair business and wanted to see how heels were put on in America.

"Mr. Burton was a bit mental," Miss Ada remarked. "Porters often are, you know. It's the odd hours they keep. I rather like the thought that Roy was a dope smuggler."

"I'm going to get up," Emily announced. "And as soon as I'm dressed Miss Ada and I are going to town for some things."

"What things? You can't drive Link's car," Henry told her.

"Link is the one who says whether I can drive or not. Link, darling, you don't mind if we take it just for a tiny little ride into Waterfall, do you? Miss Ada and I need air."

Miss Birtwistle had such a pleased look of anticipation that Link, soft-hearted guy that he was, couldn't refuse. "Take it easy on the curves, Emily," he begged.

"I'm a very careful driver. Now please let me get into my clothes."

Presently the two of them, wrapped like Eskimos in various sporting garments borrowed from Link, got into the convertible. Emily stamped on the starter, but before she could try starting in high, two cars turned into the place and disgorged a band of reporters and photographers from the most pictorial of the New York papers.

Emily received them joyfully. "Come on in," she cried, "we'll show you where it happened!"

"Are you the wife of the murdered man?" one of them demanded.

"Oh no. I only fell over the body." And she gave them a detailed account while they crowded into the living room after her. Miss Birtwistle followed, looking as happy as a bird dog.

The reporters infested the place for some time, taking pictures of Emily with another sword very much like the death weapon— Link had plenty of them—and driving Olivia into a frightened silence with their fierce and eager questions.

Before they left Emily invited them all to the studio for more pictures and further developments in the story. Then Emily and Miss Ada got into the convertible again and drove off.

They hadn't been gone more than fifteen minutes when Sergeant Fisher arrived with a crew of shovel men who went round to the back of the house and started digging a diversion channel for the stream on the other side of the pool.

Fisher came in and showed Mr. Peel and Olivia a list of recent guests at the Hotel Lexington. It was Mr. Peel who spotted the name. "Marie Dennis," he said. "Of course it couldn't be our Marie Dennis. Not a particularly unusual name."

"Marie had no plans for coming to New York," Olivia added.

"But you do know someone with this name?" Fisher asked. "A close friend? An acquaintance of Mr. Palling?"

"She's a very old and reliable friend," Olivia told him. "I've known Marie since we were children."

Fisher cleared his throat. "Any interest in your husband, do you suspect, Mrs. Palling?"

"Oh no. Marie and Roy were friendly. He admired her riding. I'm a dreadful rider myself, quite hopeless."

"So your Marie is horsy, eh? What else can you tell me about her?"

Mr. Peel described Marie critically. "Red hair, blue eyes, slender but not thin. Muscular. Has large feet."

"Oh, Father," Olivia protested, "her feet are normal."

"I think they're large," he maintained, puffing reflectively. "Rather large hands, too, for a girl. Helps to handle a horse, I imagine. Smokes."

"What brand?"

He smiled. "Anything she can get, like the rest of us. She'd be using American cigarettes here, so that won't help."

Fisher folded the list. "Where's Mrs. Bryce?" he asked suddenly. "And Miss Birtwistle?"

"They took the car for a buzz into town," Link told him. "Ought to be back any minute."

"I don't like that. I asked you all to stay within bounds."

"They've gone to buy themselves some crime magazines," Henry said easily. "They won't get into any trouble." He was wondering just what trouble they were in. They had had time to go to town three or four times. Fisher, however, was not familiar with Emily's character. He accepted the explanation and went out to boss the job on the pool.

"Do you think it is Marie?" Olivia asked her father.

"Shouldn't be at all surprised."

"But to come over and not tell us she was coming—it isn't like Marie in the least."

Link went out to watch the digging, and Henry followed him. "What do you think has happened to Emily?" Link asked.

"You'd better be wondering what's happened to your car, brother. You know Emily."

The shovels were now turning over a bed of tulips Link had put in at the expense of an aching back. He couldn't bear to watch, so they went inside again, and Link put the chicken in the pressure cooker.

Henry made corned-beef sandwiches to keep them alive till suppertime. Mr. Peel seemed to enjoy his sandwich and bottle of beer, but Olivia would eat nothing and went to her room to lie down.

"She's not strong, you know," her father said. "These young people don't eat enough. They're all nerves." Peel himself didn't look placid any more. Lines were beginning to tighten between his eyes, and his brief mustache sometimes twitched like the whiskers of a dog having a nightmare. Henry was sorry for him—he liked Peel, and it was too bad he had to go through all this muck because his daughter had been fool enough to marry Roy Palling.

"I wouldn't say this before Olivia," Peel went on hesitantly, "but I suspect Roy and Marie were not playing quite fair. She was about a great deal, you know."

"I heard only one conversation between them," Henry told him. "But I'm sure Marie had more than a friendly interest in Roy. He didn't seem to care about her, though. Just leading her on, I thought."

"Torture artist?" Link inquired.

"Exactly," Peel agreed, staring grimly into the fire. The gravity of his expression was lessened somewhat by the fact that he chewed heartily on his sandwich while he stared. He just wasn't built to play heavy tragedy. His whole nature was opposed to it.

"Maybe Marie got tired being dangled," Link suggested. "Perhaps those are Marie's big feet in the flower bed."

"Unlikely," Peel thought. "How would she get here?"

"Train and taxi," Henry suggested.

"If anybody hired a taxi to come out here last night our friend Fisher knows about it," Link pointed out. "There's only one local taxi service, and Mr. Beaman drives the car himself. He'd remember the girl."

"Maybe she came all the way from New York in a cab, as we did."

Mr. Peel swallowed the remainder of his beer, wiped his mustache on the paper napkin. "Even allowing for the vagaries of women, why should Marie come all this way to murder Roy when she might have killed him so much more easily in London?"

"And remember, she phoned him from New York. That would warn him," Henry pointed out. "Unless, of course, she was friendly over the phone, making sure he was here and ripe for the cutting."

They wondered what she had said to Roy that would compel him to walk into town to call her back.

Fisher came in, carrying a dripping black shoe.

"Roy's other boot!" Peel exclaimed.

"Damned curious idea," Fisher grunted. "No sense to throwing the fellow's clothes into the pool." He went out and tossed the object into his car, returned to the drained pool, followed by Henry, Link, and Mr. Peel.

Fisher walked through the mud and leaves that had washed in with the high water and partially covered the concrete bottom. He scanned the muck intently, going methodically up and down, while the men leaned on their shovels and watched him.

Finally the sergeant climbed out. "If there's anything else here it's mighty small," he said. "We'll have to screen the stuff on the bottom." He put the men to work. The results were five bobby pins, an old bathing cap, and a dime.

Fisher spat heartily, took his men, and departed.

Henry looked at his watch for the twentieth time. "Where do you suppose Emily is?"

"Stop worrying," Link advised. "If she's smashed up the car we'll hear about it."

A simultaneous blast of horn and screech of brakes took them to the door. Emily and Miss Ada stepped out of the convertible undamaged, each bearing an armful of Sunday papers.

"Where have you been?" Emily cried, forestalling the inquiry. "Here we sit worrying our elbows to the bone and you two driving madly around the country looking for murderers."

"I thought so," Henry retorted sternly. "Just which murderers were you looking for?"

"Vittorio." Emily smiled sweetly and entered the house. "I smell sandwiches. What were you having?"

"Never mind the red herrings. Where were you? Miss Ada, you tell the truth, I'm sure. What has my wife been up to?"

Miss Ada dropped the papers and sat down with dignity. "We made a call upon your friend Mr. Vittorio."

"You found him?" Link demanded.

"At Marble Farms," Emily interrupted. "It's a very plushy place, Link. Victorian, to go with Vittorio, I suppose. Embroidered woodwork around the porch and the windows and that sort of thing. High ceilings, dark green shutters, a marble fawn, and a fountain. A beautiful job inside, what we could see of it. Of course having all the shades down made it hard to be sure whether it was puce or gray. Remember that chandelier we sold him, Henry—the one we got from Albert the junkman and you wired some drops on it and painted it up and we made seventy-five dollars on it—well, he has that in the entrance hall. It looked lovely over his head as he stood there with the pillow."

Mr. Peel laughed, but Henry was not amused. "Emily, would you mind telling us what happened?" he ordered.

"I'm trying to. Don't you want a picture of the scene?"

"No. Did he let you in without a protest?"

"There was some delay," Miss Ada said, obviously enjoying the whole thing.

"We didn't think he was coming to the door at all," Emily continued. "In fact, we didn't think he was there. All the shutters were closed. We rang and we rang, and finally I shouted through the keyhole that it was only me. Then we heard footsteps inside—they came to the door and stopped and then they went away, and I shouted again, and finally he opened the door and there was Vittorio. What kind of sandwiches were those?" She pointed to a crust in the fireplace.

"Oh, come on, Emily," Link pleaded. "You've got your audience panting."

"At first I thought his mind was gone," Emily confessed. "He came to the door with a pillow over his head. And the house naturally was as dark as your insides, and he didn't speak. 'Oh, dear,' I thought, 'poor Vittorio. His mind is gone.' "

"Never mind what you thought," Henry put in. "What did he say?"

" 'Come in,' of course." Emily took a breath. "I was a little nervous then. I thought maybe he'd kill us, but I looked at Miss Ada and she was as cool as anything, so I was ashamed to let her know how I felt and we both went in and sat down on chairs."

"Imagine sitting on chairs," Henry said. "Did you ask him why he'd left Andersons' during the night?"

"Well, no. I didn't want to bring up unpleasant memories. You can set insane people off doing that, Henry. We just talked shop."

Mr. Peel chuckled. "What sort of shop?"

"Butcher," Link offered.

"He asked me when the chairs would be done for Parker, and I told him, vaguely, and he wants a chest like the one I did for Mrs. Emery, but I don't think I can do it until later in the season."

"You mean he talked rationally about his work, but all the time he had a pillow on his head?" Henry demanded.

"I think his talk was rational, don't you, Miss Ada?" Emily asked.

"Oh, quite. It was the cards that roused my suspicions."

Mr. Peel asked her what cards, and Miss Ada said there had been a pack of playing cards laid out on the carpet around a raw beefsteak. That, she added, had not seemed quite conventional, even for America.

"Miss Ada told his fortune with the cards," Emily said.

"It's an act," Henry decided. "He knows something happened last night and he's scared stiff he'll be involved in it, so he's playing mad." He went to the phone in the hall and called Fisher. "My wife has found Vittorio," he said.

Emily followed, protesting. "I promised we wouldn't tell anybody where he is."

Henry went on telling Fisher, and Olivia came into the hall and listened. "He must know something about last night," Henry said. "Any line yet on Marie Dennis?"

"She checked out of the Lexington at seven this morning. Now all we've got to do is find her," Fisher answered sardonically.

Miss Ada asked to speak to the sergeant. "I have a few samples for you, sir," she said modestly. "I thought perhaps you would like to be able to discover if Mr. Vittorio had been here last night without making him aware that you knew." Fisher must have asked her what kind of samples. "I told his fortune with the cards on the floor, first putting one of the cards in my pocket—the joker," she answered. "That should give you fingerprints. Then I secured a sample of the mud from the floor of his car, also mud from his own driveway. Also wool from a jacket which I found flung over the seat of his car."

Emily was regarding Miss Ada with admiration and amazement. "How did you get the mud?"

"You remember I asked him about his flowers and he told me he had beardless yellow iris. It was a natural thing for me to walk round the driveway at the side of the house to look at them."

Henry chuckled. "This comes of close study of Emily's magazines. I'm surprised you didn't take samples of lint from his trouser cuffs, Miss Ada."

"I did," she said calmly. "As I was telling his fortune I pretended I had dropped a live ash from my cigarette into his trouser turnups. It's very simple, you know, once you become familiar with what is required."

For a fraction of a second Henry had the suspicion that Miss Ada was joking, that she had no samples to give Fisher. However, when she produced a playing card and some twists of paper containing dust he wasn't sure. She was a sharp old thing, was Miss Ada. He noticed Mr. Peel regarding her with a puzzled amusement, and wondered if he had the same suspicion.

"It appears that Palling and Vittorio were tied up in some sort of deal," Link said slowly. "What do you think it was?"

"Smuggling, of course," Emily answered.

Everyone else looked skeptical, but Mr. Peel thought Emily might be on the right track. "In any case," he said, "would it not be wise to make a thorough examination of everything we brought with us from London? Roy may have used any one of us as an unconscious agent."

Olivia objected. Roy, she was sure, had had no connections of that kind.

"My dear," her father said gently, "you couldn't know all that Roy did. It occurs to me that Marie Dennis may have had a part in the game."

"Marie is not interested in money," Olivia protested. "Especially dishonest money. Horses are her whole life."

Mr. Peel raised a skeptical eyebrow. "A very expensive life."

"We're wasting time," Link said, reaching for the silver coffee-pot on the mantel. "We'll start with this, because it was near the body. Everybody bring your stuff in here and we'll go through the lot with a fine-tooth comb."

"I'm perfectly willing, of course," Miss Ada said, "but may I point out that Sergeant Fisher has already examined our luggage?"

"Perhaps he didn't have smuggling in mind," Link argued. "Anyway, it won't do any harm to have another look."

The others went to their rooms and brought back everything that had crossed the Atlantic. Link unscrewed the strawberry and leaves which formed the knob of the silver pot. He and Henry bored a hole in it with the tools Link had, none of them delicate. They succeeded in destroying the knob and found nothing whatever inside it. Henry was more hopeful of finding something in Olivia's luggage, but though they exercised great care in examining her things and Roy's nothing suspicious turned up. Mr. Peel's simple equipment yielded the same result. Miss Ada had fortified herself with every item she could possibly want from a paring knife to four pairs of pink cotton "knickers."

"They look like my old basketball bloomers," Emily commented, "except for the color. What about your knitting bag, Miss Ada?"

They turned that out, but there was only a copy of the *Deerslayer*, Miss Ada's spare set of teeth, and the gray socks on which she was knitting.

While they were eating the chicken, Conlan came to collect Miss Ada's evidence and brought the message from Fisher that they might all go into the city in the morning, providing they kept him informed of their whereabouts. Emily was vastly relieved.

Mr. Peel and his daughter and Miss Ada would put up at the Waldorf, they decided. Miss Ada generously offered to foot the bill, with the proceeds from her Pennsylvania Railroad shares, since it was unlikely that Mr. Peel could do so for any length of time on his allowed travel funds.

They asked Conlan to tell the sergeant that Vittorio was in all probability not insane, but only putting on a good show to avoid questioning.

"I'll tell him," Conlan agreed. "But don't think he misses a whisker. He knows by looking at you how many lumps of sugar you take in your coffee."

"That I find very comforting," Miss Ada remarked.

"Oh, he's good all right," Conlan assured her. "But I don't know if he's as good as Scotland Yard."

Miss Ada sniffed. "I have a relative in Scotland Yard. Cousin Bertie, one of the half-dozen genuine idiots in the family."

"Bertie is a very efficient fellow," Peel reproved.

"I'm glad to know it. I should have said he couldn't find Nelson's pillar in broad daylight."

Link decided to sleep in the living room on the sofa. "That's a very uncomfortable bed in the garage," he said.

"You're not fooling us," Emily told him. "We know you're afraid the killer might walk in its sleep."

"Emily, don't try to frighten people," Henry said sternly. "Nothing is going to happen."

"You are not in a position to know," Miss Ada pointed out, "unless you killed Roy."

Emily looked pleased at that. There was no doubt that both Miss Ada and Emily liked nothing better than being scared to death.

However, nothing did happen during the night, not even Emily's usual indigestion.

Chapter 6

Link had one fanatical idea in his generally easy nature—he insisted on catching an early train on Monday morning. He wouldn't take the car, he said—there was not room for everyone and anyway the train was quicker.

It was still dark when he rapped on their door and called to Emily and Henry, "Breakfast in ten minutes!"

Henry opened a dismal eye, saw that the rain was coming down in sheets on the terrace. Emily muttered something about the things your friends did to you and pulled on her slippers.

When they climbed into Beaman's taxi at a quarter to seven they were a sorry-looking lot, except for Link and Miss Ada, who insisted on being cheerful.

There was no real station at Waterfall—no newsstand with chocolate bars and advice on taking off fat, no bulletins on Congress worrying about the world or Wall Street worrying about Congress. Beaman sped away, leaving them to huddle under a dripping shed with a corrugated-iron roof. Olivia sneezed and Link gave her his raincoat. She was looking quite gray and miserable this morning, Henry thought.

Fortunately they didn't have long to wait. The train crawled in like a wet snake, and Miss Ada brushed off the conductor who tried to help her up the steps.

Emily's veil hung in shreds and you could have played solitaire on her lower lip. "The country," she muttered; "you can have it."

For the first half-hour there was no conversation. Each of them withdrew into his own corner, half-asleep, while the rain made channels through the dust on the train windows and the conductor plodded up and down the aisles.

At Peekskill, Emily suddenly sat forward, clutching Henry's knee. "I know where they are!" she cried.

"My nerves," Henry pleaded.

"The diamonds are in Charlie's pants!"

"Now it's diamonds. What happened to the opium?"

Mr. Peel woke up and so did Link. "How could one hide anything in those pants?" Peel asked.

"In the buttons," Emily said. "A diamond in every button. Henry, I think you should get off at 125th Street and call Roscoe or he might use the pants for a paint rag."

Henry thought Roscoe would be unlikely to open the secretary. Roscoe moved slowly on Monday morning.

The remainder of the journey was lively with speculation. They cursed the slowness of the train, argued back and forth about calling Roscoe and about what they would do with the diamonds when they had them. Emily was all for selling them and dividing the proceeds evenly. Henry said the police would have to take them. Emily said the police could have their fair cut and no more. Finally the train crept into Grand Central and the six of them hurried up the ramp, through the lower level, and out to the taxi stand. Emily snatched a cab from a Westchester broker with a sweet smile and a shove, and they tore uptown to the studio.

Henry was the first to enter. He found Roscoe getting out his brushes. "Morning, Roscoe," he said, and pulled open the drawer of the secretary. There was nothing in the drawer.

"I told you he'd use it," Emily cried. "Roscoe, where are the pants?"

"Good morning, Miss Murdock," Roscoe beamed. "You have a nice trip? How you find the feed in England, eh?"

"Where are the pants?" Henry demanded.

Roscoe shrugged. "A girl come for them early. I just get here. I am putting on my shirt when she comes in. She must be a new girl they got with Di Nobili."

"What girl?" Henry asked patiently. "Just tell me what girl took away those pants, Roscoe."

"She comes from Di Nobili. Di Nobili, she says, wants the pants from the secretary, he leaves them in there by a mistake."

"Marie," Mr. Peel said shortly. "It must have been Marie."

"Oh, Lord," Link groaned. "Wouldn't you know? If we'd caught the six o'clock, as I suggested—"

Henry said never mind that, what did this girl look like. Roscoe said she looked like anybody, he didn't pay much attention to these women. "Not good, not bad. She has a big pocketbook and she put them pants into that."

"But can't you remember anything about her?" Mr. Peel pleaded. "What color were her eyes and hair?"

Roscoe smiled good-naturedly, shrugged. "I dunno, I gotta girl." "Was she young?"

He wouldn't commit himself. She wasn't young and she wasn't old. "She talk funny," he conceded. "Like you"—he indicated Mr. Peel with a paintbrush.

"It was Marie," Miss Ada said. "Accent."

Henry wasn't so sure. Vittorio might have sent someone, a girl in the decorating business, and a number of them affected British accents. He put in a call to Fisher up in Putnam County.

Link had to open his shop. "Let me know if anything breaks," he said.

Mr. Peel and Olivia went off to register at the hotel, but Miss Ada established herself on the only empty chair and prepared to observe the decorating business.

Fisher took the disappearance of Prince Charlie's pants as a joke. He was busy looking for Marie Dennis. He had used Miss Ada's clues and they seemed to indicate that Vittorio had stepped in Link's flower bed. There were no fingerprints on the sword. Those on the kitchen doorknob appeared to be Link's.

Henry set out his brushes and cans and began work on the plaid chest. He put in about twenty minutes of patient endeavor before Mrs. Cormorant called Emily, then he was able to slip out and go down to Link's shop.

"Sit down and read all about it," Link invited, indicating the floor. There were no chairs in at the moment. "The *News* is about the best."

Henry read the large type dished out by the various gentlemen who had interviewed them the day before:

DECORATOR WITH CUTTING PIECE

—this was under a photograph of Emily with a sword, looking

like Madam Peron at a tea party.

OLD FAMILY HEIRLOOM
SLICES GUEST FROM BRITAIN
SOCIALIST LIQUIDATION SCHEME CROSSES ATLANTIC
WIPES OUT CAPITALIST
MATE MOURNS MINCED BARRISTER
COUNTRY AIR FATAL TO LONDONER

There was even a picture of Miss Ada eating a waffle, and they quoted her opinion of murder: "Useless, I should think. Everyone dies eventually."

"You know," Henry remarked, leaning against a gun display case, "I've been thinking about Marie. If she came for those pants this morning, I don't believe she killed Roy."

"Why not?" Link demanded.

"Too risky. She'd try to stay clear of the whole thing. In fact, I should think she'd want to leave the country as soon as she possibly could. Perhaps she flew out yesterday."

"The police will check that."

"If she came for the pants, she didn't even know Roy was dead," Henry decided. "Of course we're not sure she took them, but it seems possible. She must have acted on instructions from Palling first thing, before we could get to the studio."

Link agreed. "What was so valuable about those damned pants?" he wondered. "It almost looks as if Emily's lurid suspicions about smuggling were true."

"It does. But what kind of smuggling, and who was to receive the goods?"

Link thought Vittorio was the fence or the liaison man or something. "You don't suppose they'd have any correspondence about a little deal like this? No, they wouldn't. Nothing in writing. And Vittorio will probably remain out of his sweet little mind till the trouble blows over."

"Fisher will find ways of curing his madness, I imagine," Henry said. "You know, Link, all this business about the pants may be just horseplay to distract us from the real motive for the crime. I still don't understand why all these English suddenly decided to come over here."

"They figured murder was easier to get away with here," Link suggested.

A customer entered the shop, looking for a Confederate uniform, and Henry returned to the studio. Hilda Leghorn was there, having read the papers. Miss Ada had gone to the hotel, on foot, and Roscoe was out for coffee. He always went out for coffee when Hilda came.

"When I heard you were going abroad I was a little jealous," Hilda confessed, "but now I'm glad I'm only poor little me, safe and sound on Lexington Avenue."

"I feel safe," Emily protested.

"Oh, but you're not, Emily. They won't let you alone till they get what they want."

"What do they want?" Henry growled, going back to the plaid job. Hilda was Emily's best friend.

"If people get involved in a murder once in their lives, anybody would excuse it," she went on, taking one of Henry's Dunhills and striking a match near the varnish. "But when they get mixed up in another one, with foreigners, too, it almost seems too much to be a coincidence, doesn't it? I mean, these things happen more to shady characters, and if you go around minding your own business you don't seem to know murderers and things."

Emily, who could be insulted only by a crowbar, smiled brightly. "I know," she said; "isn't it interesting? And to think I probably smuggled. If it's that easy I might go into the business. By the way, Hilda, what's this about you and a big oil deal? Gottlieb was telling us."

"One can't do anything on Lexington Avenue without people spreading it around. I'd rather not talk about it yet."

"Yet? But I tell you everything, Hilda. You aren't going high-hat just over a little money, are you?"

"It will probably be a great deal of money," Hilda corrected, airily flicking ashes into a can of paint.

The suspense she had built up was spoiled by the arrival of a young man in a shapeless hat, bearing a camera. He was Mason from the *News*, he said, and would like a shot of the Bryces at work.

"Wait till I change my clothes," Emily begged, but he got a picture of her in her smock and dungarees, stiff with paint and oil. "Look," she said, "if you'll throw that one away and take me after I'm cleaned up, I'll give you some inside dirt."

"Fair enough. What's the dirt?" He leaned against the wall and looked around him. "Geez you keep a nice, tidy little place here, don't you?"

Roscoe returned, scowled at Hilda, regarded the photographer with interest, and got to work.

"This morning we all dashed into the studio looking for Charlie's pants, and what do you think?" Emily demanded. "They were gone!"

Mason's eyebrows flickered. "Who's Charlie?" he asked cautiously.

"Bonnie Prince Charlie—you know. The diamonds, everybody says, were in his pants."

"Oh. The diamonds." He was looking at her sideways now.

"You don't tell me anything about some diamonds," Roscoe complained.

"That's just a figure of speech," Emily said. "Nobody knows what I smuggled, but I like to think it was diamonds. I wouldn't want to smuggle dope, would you, Mr. Mason?"

Mason cleared his throat and looked to Henry for help. Henry merely smiled and went on painting. Mason evidently decided to take what he could get and let the boys downtown sift it for sanity. Emily changed to her black silk dress, combed her hair, and posed with a wet paintbrush.

Hilda tried to get into the picture, and when she couldn't said airily, "I'll leave you to the tabloids," and departed.

After Mason had gone, inevitably the paint and Emily's dress combined, and she said she thought she would dash down to Bloomingdale's at four o'clock to get something with a better neck to have pictures taken in.

"I thought you were going to finish Di Nobili's secretary?" Henry reminded her.

"I'll finish it. After all, Henry, publicity is important too."

"I don't know that smuggling enhances one's reputation as a decorator."

When Henry went over to the delicatessen for the sandwiches for lunch, Gottlieb said he had read what happened in the country and he hoped they weren't going to be in any trouble over it. "You keep Mrs. Bryce home," he warned. "She trusts anybody."

Henry promised to do that, but he knew he couldn't.

At two o'clock Miss Ada phoned from the Waldorf. "This hotel," she reported, "is ridiculously overfurnished. And they haven't a single open fire. Prices are shocking. Would you and Mrs. Bryce and Mr. Simpson care to dine here with me this evening?"

Henry told her the automat was plenty good enough and much cheaper.

"The point," Miss Ada stated, "is that I cannot pay cash. I shall have the proceeds from the sale of my shares tomorrow. Therefore I shall expect you here at half-past seven."

Emily was delighted. "Now I just have to get a dress," she said.

"Remember the time you rushed out to buy a dress to have lunch with Mrs. Delaphine," Henry warned. "No lunch."

"Oh, but Miss Ada is a woman of her word."

"Gottlieb thinks I ought to keep you under lock and key. He's afraid something will happen to you."

"What could happen to me in Bloomingdale's?"

At four-thirty Emily, half-assembled but bearing all the ready cash, tore out of the studio. Henry watched from the window as she crossed the avenue, turned and walked toward Fifty-ninth Street. He had an uneasy feeling about her, and half wished he'd gone along. Oh well, as Emily said, there wasn't much danger in Bloomingdale's. He went down to tell Link about the invitation from Miss Ada. Link was sorry, but he had a date.

Emily had almost decided to take the black chiffon number which made her look thin. She was studying herself in the glass when she caught a glimpse of another customer passing the booth with a clerk. They entered the next cubicle.

"Shall we try this one first, madam?" the clerk asked.

Emily waited for the answer. "Very well," the voice said crisply. No doubt about it—Marie Dennis.

Emily's clerk came back with another dress. "Maybe you'd like this one better, dear. Can you wear a draped hip?"

Emily nodded, stepped out of one dress and pulled the other over her head without saying anything.

Marie went on, "You know, I think I should prefer a brighter color—cherry perhaps."

Cherry with red hair—that would be fetching, Emily thought.

"And if you have something with ruffles, or lace, or perhaps very elaborate buttons."

"Oh, you want a dressy dress," the clerk said, and hurried away.

She's working up a disguise, Emily said to herself. She wore dark tailored clothes in London.

Emily's clerk went off to find another model, and Emily quickly got into her own dress and coat, wiped off her lipstick, and stepped around the partition.

Marie stood there in her slip. Her hair was a dandelion yellow.

"Hello," Emily said casually. "I thought I recognized your voice."

Marie collected a certain amount of disdain and spread it over her amazement. "I'm sure you've mistaken me for someone else."

"Oh, come on, Marie, I know you behind that hair. Awful bleach job. Hilda would have done it for you. Hilda's my best friend. But maybe it's just as well. Sometimes her customers lose their hair eventually. Have you a lipstick I could borrow? I'm trying to make up my mind about a dress and I think it would be easier if I had some makeup on." Emily regarded the large handbag lying on the chair with Marie's gloves. It was decidedly bulging. Marie did not move to open it. "You don't have to be afraid of me," Emily went on. "I won't give you away. Of course they are looking for you. Everybody's more or less wanted, after what happened to Roy, but I know you didn't cut him open with a sword. You'd have shot him. I really would like to borrow a lipstick, unless you believe in germs."

Marie, regarding her with a puzzled resentment, opened the bag.

Emily saw the red-and-green wool. "Charlie's pants!" she cried. "I'm so glad to find them again." She snatched the trousers and moved away.

"No, you don't," Marie said, reaching.

"I wouldn't make a noise if I were you," Emily advised, parting the curtain. "I might scream police." She hurried down the corridor and across the floor to the elevators. Marie would have to get into her clothes. The elevator was a long time coming and Emily, watching the entrance to the dressing-room corridor, saw Marie emerge. The elevator arrived, Emily stepped into it, and the doors closed, but Marie had seen her. Better get off at the next floor, Emily decided.

She found herself in the midst of a wonderful sale of girdles, and was completely absorbed by a beautiful blue satin garment marked down from $18.50 to $5.95 when she looked up and saw Marie, not ten yards away. Emily dropped the girdle and made for the escalator. She reached the street, decided she had lost Marie, and crossed to the drugstore. Feeling an urgent desire to communicate these events to someone, she entered a phone booth and dialed her own number. The phone rang in both the apartment and the studio, and Henry ought to be in one or the other. While she waited she cautiously examined the pants. The buttons were all there. Nothing seemed damaged. Was Marie such a dope she didn't know they were using the pants to smuggle with?

No one answered the phone. She dialed again. Still no answer. Henry and Link were out bending elbows. She picked up the coin, considered calling Hilda. But Hilda probably wouldn't be interested and it would involve a lot of explanation, and maybe the woman in the next booth would listen and learn that Emily had a lapful of diamonds, and that might not be healthful.

She tapped her teeth with the coin. "Mr. Peel ought to know," she decided, "and Miss Ada."

It was Miss Ada who answered. Emily told her about Marie and the pants.

"Have you looked to see if there is anything inside the buttons?" she demanded.

"No, I'm afraid to here. It's so public. I'll bring the pants when we come to dinner. Or do you think I ought to call Sergeant Fisher and give them to him?"

"He must have them eventually, I presume," Miss Ada answered. "But there's no harm in our looking at them. I advise you to take a cab to your flat. And be careful, please, Mrs. Bryce."

Emily promised to be careful, made her way to the corner of Sixtieth Street and Lexington Avenue, and found a cab. Bloomingdale's was now closing, and in any case she wouldn't have ventured back there because of the danger of meeting Marie. But she still wanted a new dress. She recalled a small dress shop in the court where Vittorio's studio was located, off Fifty-second Street, near Third Avenue. It was a private court, rather plushy, with rehabilitated old houses occupied by people who owned Great Danes and first editions. The shop would probably be expensive, but what of it, Emily reasoned, you only live once.

The owner of the Princess Olga, Modes, looked at Emily disdainfully, took a puff on her cigarette, adjusted her hat, and said, "Yes?"

"You were just closing." Emily retreated.

"Oh no," Princess Olga corrected, almost lapsing into an interest in a sale.

Emily remembered that they kept their hats on in these high-class places to show that they were in business only for the fun of it, and might take off any minute for a cocktail party. She stated her desire for a black dress, not very hopefully, as the garments draped around on wires were mostly magenta and chartreuse, with sashes. But Olga produced a nice plain black crepe, which with a little squeezing fitted Emily. She also took ten dollars off the price when Emily seemed on the point of leaving. Emily had no intention of leaving, but she thought she owed it to herself to try to get something off. She was escorted out of the shop by Olga's poodle wearing a bobby pin to keep the hair out of his eyes.

As she crossed the court she saw that there was a light in Vittorio's studio. So he had given up playing with the pillow in Putnam County and come back to town. She would just say hello, she decided, and walked up the two steps to his purple door. No one answered her knock, so she opened the door and stepped inside. Immediately the light went out.

"Hello, Vittorio," she called. "It's only me, Emily."

The space was divided into a large front room for business purposes and a small rear apartment where Vittorio lived when he wasn't using other people's houses.

Emily could hear faint breathing in the back room. This is silly, she thought, and moved toward the inner door.

"Alfredo," she called, and was surprised that her voice was shaky, "come on out and I'll show you Charlie's wonderful pants."

No answer. A pencil dropped to the floor and rolled.

"Well, if you're not receiving," she said, trying to sound jaunty, and turned around. At that moment the inner door opened and something shot past her, hit the floor with a crackle of broken glass. Emily reached the door in two steps, yanked it open, and ran. She didn't stop till she reached Lexington Avenue, where she fell into a cab and gasped, "Sixty-second, please."

"Anything the matter, lady?" the driver asked.

"I always get out of breath when I run," Emily told him. "Cold for April, isn't it?"

"I thought the cops was on your tail."

"Do you think $18.50 is too much for a girdle?"

"It's more than I'd pay, lady, but I don't wear a girdle. Would anybody be following you?"

"I don't think so." Emily turned and gazed out the back window at the bouncing lights tearing along behind them. "Why?"

"I thought maybe you'd like me to lose 'em, if they was."

"Oh. If you want to, go ahead and lose them."

"Okay." He suddenly shot west on Fifty-seventh, continued to Fifth Avenue, drove into the park, and bowled along between the lamplighted trees. "I think we done it," he said, grinning around at her. "Home now?"

"Home, James," Emily agreed, relaxing slightly.

She climbed the stairs to the apartment, hoping Henry would be there. Theirs was the rear apartment on the second floor. The halls were dark again. The stinking landlord, Emily muttered, always saving a tenth of a cent an hour. She knocked first, and when Henry didn't open the door she groped in her full handbag for the key, found it, and fitted it into the lock. There was a sound behind her, soft as a bird flying. She had no time to turn.

Henry expected to find Emily, but not on the floor. He had come up the stairs rather carefully, grumbling at the landlord for neglecting the hall lights, pulled out his keys, knocked loudly, and then unlocked the door.

He almost fell over Emily as he stepped into the foyer and reached for the light switch. She lay quite near the door, on her back. Her hat had fallen off and rolled near her handbag, which was open.

He knelt beside her, frightened, and felt her forehead. Warm. She wasn't dead. He rubbed her wrists, shook her gently. She moved.

"Emily," he said sharply, "wake up!"

Her eyes opened.

"Hello, Henry." She looked at him vaguely.

He got her some brandy, propped her up while she sipped it.

"What happened to me?" she demanded.

"That's what I'm asking you. I came up expecting to see you trying on a new dress, and here you were on the floor."

She remembered. As she put the key in the lock, something hit her on the back of the head. "The taxi driver thought somebody was following me," she said. "We went through the park to lose him."

"You'd better lie down awhile. Can you get over to the sofa?"

"I've been lying down," Emily pointed out. "Is there any more brandy?"

He didn't think she ought to have more before dining with Miss Birtwistle. "Or would you rather not go to the Waldorf now?"

"Not go? After I've bought a new dress and everything?" Emily got to her feet, sat down rather suddenly in the nearest chair. "I feel a little funny," she admitted. "Where's my bag? Was I robbed?"

Henry shook the contents of the bag onto the table at her elbow. "My wallet's gone," she said. "I thought they only wanted the pants."

"Pants?" Henry raised his eyebrows. "Sure you won't lie down?"

"Charlie's pants, dope. I got them away from Marie while she was helpless in her underwear. Then I went to Vittorio's——"

"Wait. You saw Marie? Where?"

"In Bloomingdale's, of course. I didn't know her at first because she's had her hair bleached, Henry. A ghastly job. Hilda couldn't do worse."

"You actually saw Marie in Bloomingdale's? What did she do?"

"She ran after me, as soon as she could get her dress on. But I was in the elevator and she was outside when the doors closed, so I got off in a sale of girdles. I saw the most beautiful blue satin number, Henry, marked down from $18.50 to $5.95. And I couldn't buy it because just then I looked up and saw Marie, with murder in her eye. Why do you always see a bargain at a time like that? When I was on the way to the hospital with poor Uncle Gregory and his appendix we passed Peck & Peck's summer sale and of course I couldn't get out of the cab."

"Marie had Charlie's pants, and you took them away from her," Henry said, trying to clear away some of the underbrush. "Then what?"

"Then Miss Ada said I'd better take a cab and come right home. I still didn't have a dress—"

"How did Miss Ada happen to be in Bloomingdale's at this psychological moment?"

"She wasn't, Henry." Emily looked exasperated. "I phoned them when I couldn't get you, because I knew they'd like to know I had the pants."

"One of them, apparently, was delighted to know."

Emily was indignant. "You know they wouldn't hit me. They aren't that kind of people."

"No? They don't object to cutting throats."

"Anyway, Miss Ada was the only one who knew. Mr. Peel and Olivia weren't there." Emily frowned, trying to assemble what had happened to her in an orderly fashion—a process she found difficult at best. "Vittorio might have followed me from his studio. I went in there, Henry, and he threw something at me from the back—from his apartment. And he didn't say a word. I bought a dress in Olga's shop—in his court, you know. So then it seemed silly not to say hello to Vittorio and see if he was still out of his mind. I guess he is. It was quite a heavy vase he threw. He could have hurt me."

Henry digested these facts as best he could. He asked Emily if she had seen Vittorio, and she said no.

"You didn't see him or hear him. How do you know it was Vittorio?"

"I never thought of that, Henry. Suppose Marie was in there, poking around?"

Marie, Henry thought, was the least likely person to have been there. He was thinking of Mr. Peel and Olivia. One of them might have been engaged in searching Alfredo's apartment when Emily ventured into the studio. They wouldn't want her to know they were there, and the best way to get her out was to frighten her. He suggested this to Emily, but she rejected the idea as absurd.

"What would Olivia or Mr. Peel want from Vittorio?" she demanded.

"Well, suppose Vittorio and Roy were in a big smuggling deal. Vittorio might have the articles they smuggled."

"The jewels?" Emily asked, making it concrete. "But everybody knows the jewels were in Charlie's pants."

"But until you found Marie, no one knew where the pants were."

"That's so. I like Olivia as a smuggler. Olivia and Vittorio. They killed Roy to have more of the loot. Then Olivia decided to take it away from Vittorio."

Henry snorted. "Did you say anything when you were in Vittorio's studio? Anything about the pants, I mean?"

"Of course. I told him I wanted to show him the pants."

"Oh. That makes it more interesting. Whoever was in the studio could also be the person who followed you here and knocked you out. Why you want to go broadcasting everything to everybody is a great mystery to me, Emily." Henry turned on all the lights and began looking behind chairs.

"You don't think he's still here?" Emily asked fearfully.

"I think the pants are here," he said, and bending down behind one of the Victorian armchairs he came up with them.

"Aren't you clever!"

Henry looked them over. Some of the buttons were gone, but not all. He dug in Emily's scrambled sewing basket for scissors.

"Do you realize it's after seven, Henry?" Emily demanded. "I haven't even got my mink out of moth balls. You can take the trousers apart when we get there."

The fur cape Emily had acquired after the murder of Mrs. Delaphine was becoming a little shabby, but still, as Emily said, an old mink had more impact than a new muskrat.

In twenty minutes they were on their way, Emily tying her pearls and zipping her zipper in the cab. "Do you think the buttons with the diamonds in them are gone?" she asked.

"Probably."

"Are you going to search their rooms when we get there?"

"Wouldn't find anything."

"I wouldn't be surprised if they turned up under a potted palm."

"They don't have potted palms."

"Maybe under glass, then, with the guinea hen."

Emily enjoyed walking through the Waldorf. She took in everything, moving her head from side to side as she passed between the chairs and sofas. Probably, Henry reflected, she saw every third person as a spy, an opium eater, or a numbers king. He stopped at the cigar counter, bought Dunhills and Virginia Rounds. Miss Ada seemed to approve of Virginia Rounds. It occurred to Henry that Miss Ada might possibly have taken more than one while she was at the Andersons'. Austerity created odd habits in the best people. It also occurred to him that the cigarette he had found in the rock garden might have been hers rather than Vittorio's. But that didn't make anything clearer.

Miss Ada was doing it up brown. She had ordered drinks sent up, and had remembered Henry's and Emily's preference for whiskey with ice.

"Now," she said, as soon as everyone was properly holding a glass, "let's see these remarkable trousers, Mrs. Bryce."

Emily took them out of Henry's coat pocket. "I'm afraid you're going to be disappointed. Because after I talked to you somebody followed me home and hit me on the head and cut some of the buttons off these things. But maybe they didn't have time to cut the right buttons. Have you a scissors?"

Olivia quickly produced a pair, and it was she who snipped off the buttons and cut the plaid covering of each one as she did so. The button was composed of a wooden disk padded with cotton and covered with the material of the trousers. Some of the disks were broken.

Henry watched the faces of their three friends. Miss Ada appeared interested but not excited. Mr. Peel puffed impassively on his pipe. They might have worn those same expressions had they been watching someone carve a turkey. Olivia, on the other hand, was excited. Her hands shook as she cut threads, and she kept talking. Olivia didn't ordinarily talk much.

"Not in this one," she said. "Perhaps these larger buttons on the legs. Do you see any reason, Mr. Bryce, for leaving the trousers in your apartment?"

Henry said he supposed no one wanted to be caught with them. They were rather bulky to conceal.

"Are you absolutely sure you didn't see this person who attacked you?" Olivia asked, looking very hard at Emily.

"I didn't have time to see anything," Emily assured her. "Bang-crash, I was out."

"This is the last button," Olivia announced in a moment. "If it isn't here, we simply don't have it."

"Of course," her father reminded her, "there is the rather strong possibility that there never was anything in any of those buttons."

"Then they could have let my head alone," Emily grumbled. "Although it does feel a lot better after the drink." She gave Miss Ada a hopeful glance, and Miss Ada passed her the bottle.

Henry had been counting, and he wondered how long Emily would be with them in spirit, but he didn't say anything. His first wife had always counted his drinks and he'd found it a spur to drinking. He didn't want Emily to be silly, but she was entitled to a little fun after her rough experience. And what was a slight intoxication compared with slitting a man's throat? He felt the chances were very good that one of these people had done that.

They left nothing but ice in the glasses and went down to dinner. Miss Ada took along her eternal knitting bag, in which she carried her knitting and a quantity of Kleenex, an American product that seemed to impress her.

Mr. Peel started slightly as they entered one of the smaller dining rooms. Sitting near the orchestra platform, stuffing his face with evident enjoyment, was Alfredo Vittorio.

He saw them at once and rose, waving a chicken leg. "Emily darling!" he cried.

Henry was embarrassed, but Emily just said, "Hello, Alfredo," and walked on.

"The gentleman asked for your table, Mr. Peel," the headwaiter told him sternly.

"Indeed?" Peel smiled, undisturbed. "He is not one of our party."

Vittorio watched them being seated, his face too sad even for one about to be hung. Suddenly he threw down his napkin and the chicken leg, pushed back his chair, and steered over.

"Emily, my love, are you angry with me? What have I done? Just tell me, what have I done?"

Emily looked at him. "You've dribbled on your vest."

Vittorio looked down at his glistening shirt front. He was wearing a dinner jacket and was conventionally garbed from head to foot except for a hand-painted tie embroidered with sequins. The other customers were watching with interest, and Henry felt as though he had been caught naked in Tiffany's.

Miss Ada leaned toward Alfredo, picked something off his right sleeve. "Green," she said cryptically, and laid a short thread on the tablecloth.

Vittorio gave her an uncomprehending stare and refocused on Emily.

"Why did you throw that glass thing at me?" she inquired without bitterness. "You might have hurt me. And when you hit me on the head, why did you have to drag me into the apartment and snag my stockings?"

Vittorio's expression was one of complete bewilderment. "Emily darling, you know I wouldn't hurt you for anything in the world. What is all this? Explain. I'm crazy—I admit I'm crazy—but not dangerous." His own words seemed to remind Vittorio that he was supposed to be out of his mind. Abruptly he returned to his table, hung his napkin over his head, and picked up the chicken leg. The headwaiter followed, clucking.

"Miss Ada, what was that about a green thread?" Emily demanded.

"I imagined it was the same sort of thread with which some of the buttons were sewed on those famous trousers," Miss Ada told her.

"Really?" Emily stared at Alfredo. "Then he must be the person who knocked me out and cut off the buttons."

Mr. Peel pursed his lips. "One ought not to jump to conclusions. Perhaps it is not the same thread. Looks a bit new to me." He regarded it judicially as it lay on the white linen cloth.

Emily said it was easy to find out. She produced the trousers, which she had carried to dinner rolled in her cape. This new development caused a stir at the next table. Emily, unaware of it, held Miss Ada's green thread against the snipped threads on one of the ankles. It did look very much the same.

Henry glanced across the room at Alfredo, but he was taking no interest in them now. He had apparently finished his dinner, for he rose and made his way out with dignity, the napkin having been removed from his head by a waiter.

Henry excused himself and followed him through the lobby and down the steps on the Lexington Avenue side. Alfredo paused to light a cigarette, and Henry stepped up behind him, pressed a finger into his spine, and snarled, "Don't move."

Alfredo gave out a sound like someone trying to scream in a nightmare, withered, sank against the wall. Henry hadn't counted on anything so complete. He didn't quite know what to do, with people passing and Alfredo sinking nearer and nearer the pavement. He stopped a cab, explained that his friend was a bit tight, asked for help.

The driver came round and the two of them helped the frightened and unwilling Alfredo to a seat in the vehicle. "Where are you taking me, Bryce? What are you doing with me? I don't know anything."

"Take it easy, Alfredo," Henry said gently. "We'll just go round to my apartment for some black coffee. Straighten you out in no time."

"I tell you, I'm not tight. I'm perfectly sober. I had nothing to drink this evening."

Henry leaned forward and gave the driver the Sixty-second Street address. As they passed the studio he saw a light in Link Simpson's shop. "Wait," he said. "I think we'll get out here."

The driver, relieved, said okay. Henry grasped Alfredo's arm as he descended. "We'll just say hello to Simpson," he urged, leading him to the door of the antique shop.

Link was sitting at his desk mournfully going over his bills, and he greeted Henry with enthusiasm. "I didn't have a date after all, it seems. Who's your little frightened friend?"

"You know Alfredo."

"Used to, but he's turned so pale. Sit down, brother, before you faint."

Vittorio stuck out his lower lip and sat heavily on a French gilt chair. "My nerves cannot go much further." He held out a trembling hand for them to see.

"I thought we'd have a talk with Alfredo," Henry explained, "and find out what he knows about some red-and-green pants and the stuff that was smuggled into the country with them. Also, who is actually doing the smuggling. First it would be logical to search him, don't you think so?"

"By all means," Link agreed. "We wouldn't want him to be embarrassed, so I'll put up a screen." He unfolded a musty leather affair around the protesting Vittorio while Henry removed the decorator's coat, shirt, pants, and shoes. Alfredo, sitting there in his shorts with his fat white chest and stomach exposed, looked as if he were going to cry.

While Link and Henry were busily going through the pockets of the jacket, Vittorio quietly put his hand on one of the old swords on the shelf behind him. Henry caught the movement and Vittorio's hand.

"He's soft but he's sly," Link remarked, tapping Vittorio's jelly-like chest. "Keep sharp things out of the baby's reach."

They read everything they found in his pockets, but none of it was helpful. "He's burned any letters he had from Jerome, anyway," Henry observed. "And if it was smuggling, they didn't put it in writing."

Alfredo gave out a long sigh and said nothing.

"What about his studio? He may have papers there," Link suggested.

Alfredo smiled. "You perhaps have never heard of an organization called the police?"

"Fisher searched your studio, eh?" Henry asked. "Find anything? No, or you wouldn't be at large. You know, Link, Alfredo was dining at the Waldorf and by a strange coincidence in the very dining room where we were expected. In fact he had asked about Mr. Peel's table. You don't think he wants to get in touch with one of them, do you?"

"Rather public," Link objected.

"Looks more innocuous that way. But they don't want to get in touch with him, apparently. Which one is it, Alfredo? Is it Olivia? Is it Miss Birtwistle? Or is it Mr. Peel?"

Alfredo's expression as Henry mentioned the three names remained uniformly pained. They asked him how the green thread had come to be on his coat sleeve, and he said he had no idea what they were talking about. Henry told him it matched some thread that appeared to be rather important in the case.

Vittorio smiled. "That old lady is no fool," he said. "She pretended to find a thread on me. She had it all the time." He began to shiver, and they allowed him to put on his clothes. Vittorio might be a criminal but he would never be hardened. He asked if he might go home now and rest, and they let him out.

Link left the door open to get rid of the smell of hair oil and mignonette. "You know, Henry," he said, tapping his desk with a small rusty dagger, "if old Alfredo had been busy cutting Roy's throat up in the country, we'd have smelled that mignonette around the living room."

Henry wasn't sure. They had been so startled at finding Roy that perhaps any strange odors would have gone unnoticed. There was always a heavy fragrance of burned pine from the fireplace, and the porch door had been open. Alfredo's perfumes would have been rather quickly dissipated.

"I don't really believe he could cut a throat, do you?" Link asked.

"He reached for a sword just now. I suspect his strawberry-jello exterior is deceptive. But our friend Fisher apparently hasn't got anything on him or he'd be in jail."

Henry told Link about Marie and the royal pants in Bloomingdale's, and how these same pants had been relieved of their buttons while Emily lay unconscious on the floor. "I didn't want to tell you all this in front of Alfredo, in case he didn't know it already."

"Emily thought Alfredo followed her home and knocked her out?"

"She didn't actually see him in his studio, but she assumed he was there. Of course it may have been Marie who followed Emily home and cut the buttons off the trousers. But why didn't she do that while she had them?"

Link thoughtfully picked his teeth with the dagger.

"Marie didn't know what the whole thing was about. Somebody, presumably Roy, told her to go and get the pants from your studio, but when she had 'em she didn't know what to do with 'em. Sometime during the day, apparently not very early, she read about Roy's murder and decided to change her appearance. Then Emily came along and snatched the pants and Marie got the idea that there was something valuable hidden in them. She can't get out of the country, can she?"

Henry didn't see how. She'd have to use her own name, since that was on her passport, and if Fisher had her posted at the airport and with the shipping companies she would have a difficult time leaving. But she still had the whole United States to roam through.

"Why didn't she leave town this morning?" Link wondered.

"She didn't know about Roy's murder this morning. You know how women are—never read a paper if they have anything better to do. Maybe she read the *Times*. They had Roy back among the dead railroad presidents. Emily says she's had her hair bleached. Maybe while she was having that done she got around to the *News* or the *Mirror*, and found out she had a part in a gory piece of news."

Link objected. Why should Marie have the color of her hair changed before she knew she was likely to be hunted in connection with Roy's death?

"That's right," Henry admitted. "She isn't the type to have her hair bleached for fun—probably considers it vulgar. Therefore she's frightened. Either she killed Roy herself, or she doesn't want to be picked up as a witness. She may know who killed him. Have you thought of that?"

"I still say she would leave town in either case."

Henry said it was easier to hide in New York. "I wonder how she was able to locate Roy at your place?"

Link nodded toward Gottlieb's brightly lighted windows across the street. "Did you tell the cheesecake king?"

"That's it. She found our address in the phone book, came to the neighborhood, and asked around."

They strolled over to Gottlieb's and that gentleman said yes, he remembered a red-haired young lady with a strange accent. "I told her you went up to the country," he explained. "She wanted to know how to get there, and I said I don't know, lady, I never been above Sixty-ninth Street, but I think you got to take a train."

"What did she say then?" Link asked.

"She wanted to know how much it would cost. How do I know?"

"Short of funds," Henry remarked. "That may be why she doesn't leave the city. I wonder if she actually went up to Waterfall?"

"Let's hope she did, and killed the guy. I rather like your other friends."

Henry smiled. "Especially Olivia, eh?"

"Miss Ada's my favorite."

"You don't fool me, brother. By the way, what happened to your date tonight?"

"We had a slight altercation." Link grinned.

"Again? Sometimes I think you're going to marry that repulsive blonde. Come on back to the party with me. You were invited, you know."

With a little persuasion, Link came along.

When they reached the hotel they found that the party had gone upstairs. Emily opened the door of the suite.

"Guess what?" she cried. "The joint's been cased."

"Would you mind speaking English?" Henry asked.

"You tell him, Mr. Peel," Emily requested. "They never believe me."

Peel smiled. "One or two things appear to have been disturbed," he said. "Namely the whiskey bottle, my other trousers, and Cousin Ada's dressing case."

"It could not have been the maid," Miss Ada put in promptly. "We asked her. George says he always hangs his trousers by the waistband, but they were hung by the legs. I could see at once that things in my alligator case had been shuffled about. But the one piece of certain evidence was my bottle of Eno's Fruit Salts. Someone had opened it and spilled some of the salts on the washbasin. I shouldn't be at all surprised if he took a dose."

"Fisher?" Henry suggested.

"He had every opportunity to search our things at Mr. Simpson's house," Olivia reminded him.

Link said they could at any rate be sure it wasn't Vittorio. It could have been Marie, but he didn't see how any ordinary citizen could enter their suite without permission. The locks were good and there were dozens of employees about. "More likely it was the police," he added. "Although you wouldn't expect them to try Miss Ada's medicine."

"Where did you leave Alfredo's body?" Emily asked.

"We let him live," Link told her. "Your husband searched him in my place of business. He looks just the way you'd think he would look naked."

Olivia shuddered slightly. "Horrid man. I can't imagine Roy doing business with him." She gave Link one of her pale and charming smiles, and Henry could see it dissolving his gizzard.

They all had a nightcap, then Emily rolled up the royal trousers, flung on her mink jacket, and said, "Come on, I've got to work in the morning."

Link looked doubtfully at Olivia. "I don't suppose you would consider having lunch with me tomorrow, Mrs. Palling?"

"I'm afraid that would be impossible," she said gently.

"Don't be a conventional fool, Olivia," Miss Ada urged. "No one will be the wiser." Mr. Peel agreed with her, and so Olivia accepted.

Henry mulled this over as he and Emily and Link rode down in the elevator. Olivia's husband was lying on a marble slab and Olivia was gaily making luncheon dates with brand-new men. He didn't know, but he thought Link ought to be careful.

"Suppose," he began tactfully, as the three of them walked up Lexington Avenue in the cool spring evening, "the *Mirror* gets a shot of you and Olivia having martinis in Joe's?"

"He won't take Olivia to Joe's, Henry. What are you thinking of?"

"The Plaza then. So much the worse. The police may get the idea Link knocked off her husband." He stopped to light a cigarette, went on, "Anyway, Olivia is suffering from shock. She doesn't know what she's doing."

Link laughed. "You mean if she were in her right mind she wouldn't make a date with me?"

"I didn't say that."

"You're probably right, Henry. What would a girl like Olivia see in me?"

Henry had never known Link to be so humble where a female was concerned. It was embarrassing to find him softening up like this.

"Who is she?" Emily sniffed. "Bluebeard's mother for all we

know. And why shouldn't she be interested in you, Link? Where would she find a nicer, kinder, dopier meal ticket than you?"

"Thanks," Link said. "But her father appears to be a prosperous gent, and obviously Olivia will get all he has."

"After taxes," Henry said.

They stopped at the mink-coat automat for a cup of coffee. Henry took an envelope from his pocket and said he wanted to see the trousers again.

"Don't be dramatic," Emily begged, handing him the pants. "It's after midnight. I'm tired."

Henry shook a bit of wood from the envelope and compared it with one of the button molds. It appeared to be a piece of a similar button mold.

"We're supposed to ask him where he got it," Link muttered.

"I'm not asking anything," Emily said flatly. "If he wants to let us in on it, I'll listen for three minutes. Do you suppose they have any chocolate pie left?"

Link went over to see, returned with butterscotch pecan and a gob of whipped cream.

Emily revived. "I could listen for three and a half minutes now, if you want to be Sergeant Fisher," she said to Henry.

"I found this little piece of wood in their bathroom," Henry explained.

"In Mr. Peel's bathroom?" Emily demanded, through pecans.

"Mr. Peel's and Olivia's and Miss Ada's."

"What does that give us?" Link wanted to know.

"It gives us Miss Ada as a suspect," Henry suggested. "Trying to pin things on Alfredo by finding that green thread on his sleeve."

"Don't leave out Olivia," Emily reminded him. "Or Mr. Peel. But maybe the man who took the salts dropped the piece of wood."

"Maybe," Henry agreed. "If not, one of them went into the bathroom for privacy to examine the buttons he had cut off Charlie's pants. He thought he had carefully gathered and disposed of any odd bits of wood, cotton, or cloth, but this piece escaped his eye."

"Olivia's not nearsighted," Link said quickly.

"Neither are Miss Ada and Mr. Peel," Emily put in, but Henry didn't think she knew.

"Perhaps Miss Ada is protecting one of the others," Link suggested. "She may think one of them did it."

Henry agreed. "In fact, she may know one of them did it."

Emily said it couldn't be Miss Ada, and Link said it couldn't be Olivia, and Henry didn't think it was Mr. Peel, so that left nobody. Emily finished her pie and they went on.

They asked Link to come up for a drink, and Henry was glad he said no. It had been a very long day. Henry yawned as they entered their apartment, made his way blindly to the bathroom, and groped for his toothbrush.

"Henry!" Emily cried.

He dropped the toothbrush, swore mildly, got down on his hands and knees to get it from under the tub.

"They've been here," she announced, flinging open the door. "They've been at the brandy. And they used one of our best glasses!"

He got up, finished brushing his teeth, and went silently out to inspect the premises. The brandy bottle and glass stood on the coffee table in front of the red-and-white striped couch. The imprint of a seated human form showed on the couch and on the cushion against the wall. There was a cigarette in the ashtray. It was one of Henry's own.

"Probably just that drunk from upstairs," Henry grunted. "Helped himself."

"You know he couldn't get in with the door locked. Do you suppose the same person was here and in their rooms at the Waldorf?"

"If it was the same person, who could it be? Link and I had Alfredo in the shop. You were with Miss Ada and Mr. Peel and Olivia. There's only one person left—Marie."

Emily shrugged. "I don't think Marie has the brains to search apartments and hotel rooms. Do you?"

Henry didn't know Marie well enough to say. It seemed to him more likely that the police had been in both places.

Chapter 7

Emily showed no inclination to get up the next morning. Henry gave her various encouraging bulletins on the time, the weather, and the exciting possibilities in connection with Roy's murder. She didn't move a muscle, so Henry dressed, left a glass of tomato juice on the table beside her, and went over to Gottlieb's for bacon and eggs.

Link was already there, blinking through the *Tribune*.

"Have any bright ideas during the night?" Henry asked, unfolding the *Times*.

"Nothing startling, I'm afraid. If one of our friends at the Waldorf found the right buttons on Charlie's pants, there won't be any more looking for hidden treasure, will there?"

Henry didn't know. Somebody had been looking for something in their apartment last night, he said.

"Button, button, who's got the button?" Link buttered one of Gottlieb's hot rolls and ate it slowly. "Has it occurred to you, my boy, that whatever it is they're all looking for may never have been in those pants at all?"

"Then why knock Emily out to get them?"

"At that time the knocker-out didn't know. He found out later and thought maybe you and Emily had removed the goods, so he searched your apartment."

Henry said it was someone who knew he had plenty of time— he had sat there calmly sipping brandy while he thought over the world's problems.

"Is Marie much of a drinker?" Link asked.

"She likes her liquor."

Link had a dreamy look. Thinking about lunch with Olivia, no doubt. Presently he said, "Don't shoot till you hear from me," and got up, leaving his paper behind.

If the thing they were all looking for had never been in the trousers, Henry reflected, could it still be up at Link's place in the country? Could one of those three charming people—or Roy—have decided that that was the safest place for it? Meanwhile all the others were still searching.

Gottlieb came over and refilled his coffee cup from a big granite pot. He had no truck with these effete glass coffee makers. "Nice day," he said. "I am saving some apple crumb cake for Miss Murdock." He always called Emily Miss Murdock—having had a hard time learning the name in the first place he wasn't going to discard it for a mere husband. His pleasant face suddenly took on a look of patient suffering. Hilda Leghorn had come in.

"Give me a cup of coffee, Fritz, if it's fresh." Hilda knew he hated to be called Fritz.

"My coffee is always fresh," Gottlieb told her.

She sat down across from Henry and he immediately put the *Times* between them.

"I told Emily if she married you all she'd get would be a pair of legs and a newspaper in the morning. Isn't it funny how men never can be polite at breakfast? I feel sociable in the morning, don't you, Mr. Gottlieb?" She turned around to scan the well-loaded counter and glass case, and her wrinkled nose discounted the quality of the pecan rolls, the fruity coffee rings, the cheesecake, the round pats of butter, the little paper cups of marmalade, peach, and strawberry jam, the apple strudel. "Do I want anything with my coffee? I don't think so. Nothing appeals to me. I wish you'd get something interesting for breakfast, Fritz."

Henry tried not to listen. He read McCreery's ad for corduroy crawlers with removable plastic panty, reached the personal column, went through the first item without understanding it, read it again.

M.D. Please communicate
with your compatriots who
wish to help you

Uncle Box 401 Times

He read it for the third time. M.D. could be Marie Dennis. Uncle

could be George Peel. Although he was not her uncle, that was
what she called him. Was Peel trying to find Marie before the police located her? He wondered what the chances were of her reading this particular column in this particular paper. Curious, he
opened the *Tribune* but found no similar ad there. Uncle seemed
very confident that M.D. would read the *Times*.

Henry ate his breakfast, turned a deaf ear to Hilda, who pep-
pered him with questions about the great mystery.

"I'll ask Emily," she said finally. "She can't keep anything to
herself. Thanks for being so sweet." She switched her nervous
rear out of the place, and Henry and Gottlieb settled into friendly
silence. Henry took out an envelope and wrote on it:

> *Dear Uncle:*
> *Will be glad to meet you in back of library (Bryant*
> *Park) at 9 P.M.*
>
> *M.D.*

He could try it. If Uncle didn't get a genuine letter from M.D. he
might be fooled by this one and turn up, and Henry could see who
wanted to get in touch with Marie. Of course there was a very
strong possibility that the ad had nothing whatever to do with either Mr. Peel or Marie.

Miss Birtwistle was up at seven and in the dining room at ten minutes before eight. The waiter, who was an utter fool and treated her
as if he feared she would topple at any moment, brought her the
New York *Times* and the menu. She put on her glasses and studied the latter while he made inane remarks about the weather in
England.

"I don't suppose you have any kipper?" she demanded, not looking at him.

"I believe we have, ma'am. I'm sure we have. What else, ma'am?
Some grapefruit? Very nice this morning. Or prunes. The prunes
are nice."

"I never eat fruit for breakfast," Miss Birtwistle stated in tones
that ought to indicate to the creature what gastronomic folly lay in

that direction. "Coffee with hot milk, toast, and marmalade." She thrust the menu at him and picked up the newspaper, which was a formidable size, composed largely of advertising and detailed despatches from parts of the world nobody cared a farthing for anyway. Earthquake in Peru. Now, really, couldn't they keep their earthquakes to themselves? Must one have these distant disasters with one's breakfast? A belch in Siam was televised, amplified, and analyzed as a critical factor in foreign policy. The world was become a stuffy little room in which one had to share the universal toothache.

She glanced about impatiently for her waiter, but he was not in sight, so she went on reading. What some idiot of a government official thought about the world situation. As if a government official could think anything worth printing. A place called Macy's was selling something called an "uplift strapless bra." Interesting. She wondered how it functioned. Perhaps it would be an outlet for stays. Cousin Bertie's family had had investments in stays. Dividends had fallen off because of these new elastic garments. Frightfully unhealthful, obviously.

The kipper arrived, rather dry but not bad. She felt the waiter's eyes on her as she ate the bones. Irritated, she opened the paper and held it in front of her. There was some advertising of the type one sometimes found on the front page of the London *Times*, about people's dogs dying and memorials to long-lost spouses and such things. The first item read:

M.D. PLEASE COMMUNICATE
WITH YOUR COMPATRIOTS WHO
WISH TO HELP YOU

UNCLE BOX 401 TIMES

Miss Birtwistle swallowed a mouthful of herring and choked.

The waiter poured more water into her glass, looked as if he were about to pound her back. "If you put your arms over your head, ma'am," he suggested.

"I know how to cough, young man," Miss Birtwistle snapped. M.D., she was thinking, might be Marie. And Uncle might be

Cousin George. If so, what was the poor, misguided fool up to now? She stopped coughing, turned to the waiter. "How does one answer an advertisement like this?" she inquired, pointing.

It took some time for him to digest the question and the printed matter. "I guess you write a letter," he said finally.

"And where would one collect the answers?"

He scratched his ear with the napkin he carried. "Maybe you would go there and say you wanted 'em. They got an office some-place, I think."

"I imagine they have," Miss Birtwistle agreed. "How long does it take a letter to be delivered in this city?"

"That depends on your luck," he said. "My sister mailed me a letter from Brooklyn, right at Borough Hall, and you know how long it took me to get that letter? Five days."

"Shocking," Miss Birtwistle said. "I presume that was exceptional service?"

"Yes, ma'am. Generally they get there in one day."

In that case, she thought, if M.D. answers Uncle the letter will be at the *Times* office tomorrow morning. I shall go and ask for it before George is up. That will prevent one false move, at any rate. Suppose someone were to deliver the answer by hand, today? I doubt if that will occur to George. I shall go there today.

George was utterly transparent. One could predict his reactions as easily as those of Cousin Bertie. She didn't know why she kept thinking of Bertie. That little man at the cigar counter yesterday reminded her of him. He had vanished before she could approach near enough to see his face. He was short, round, and doughy, and he wore a bowler hat and spats. In London he would have melted into any crowd, but here he seemed oddly conspicuous. Miss Ada recalled a song of her youth, "Rats, rats, in bowler hats and spats, in the quartermaster's store." But Bertie was not a rat in any sense of the word. Merely a plodding, ordinary little man.

She finished her breakfast, put the paper under her arm and, correct in her surmise that the waiter would be too timid to ask her for it, sailed slowly out of the room.

At the elevators she met Olivia, who had come down in hat and coat. "Good morning, dear," Olivia said, giving her the conventional peck on the cheek which Miss Ada detested. "I see you've bought the *Times*. Could I see it a moment?"

"They'll give you one in the dining room."

"Oh, I've had breakfast."

Miss Ada pursed her lips. She saw no reason for breakfast in one's room unless one were an invalid. She handed the paper to her niece, who turned aside and quickly opened it to the page containing the item about M.D. and Uncle. Miss Ada could not be certain, but it appeared that Olivia read that item. Then she returned the paper, smiled mechanically, and said, "Thank you. I shan't see you until dinner, Cousin Ada. Have a nice day."

"I fail to see how a luncheon can take the whole day."

Olivia flushed. "I don't expect it will take my whole day. While we're here, I thought I might see some of the shops."

"You have no money. If you care to accompany me to the broker's office I could supply you with a modest sum."

Olivia said that was very sweet, but she really had no need of money, she did not intend to buy a thing, and business offices were a frightful bore. "Unless you really need me," she added more thoughtfully.

"Indeed not," Miss Ada said promptly. "I'm quite able to get about by myself." Olivia gave out one or two more polite phrases coined particularly for relatives and other nuisances and hurried away. Olivia had changed, Miss Ada thought, watching her as she wove skillfully through the little knots of people toward the steps. It had taken her no time at all to lose that cowed look, to straighten her shoulders, thicken her lipstick, change her hair, and assume an altogether different manner toward the world. Remarkable, Miss Ada said to herself. Truly remarkable. And a flicker of suspicion crossed her mind. One could be quite wrong, she admitted. But Olivia loved clothes and was utterly weak where hats were concerned. Only an errand of great importance would cause her to refuse this opportunity to indulge in an American creation.

George stepped out of an elevator. "Well, well, up with the dawn, eh?" He smiled. "I'm an old lazybones. Olivia's gone shopping. Did her a world of good to have an invitation for luncheon. Not the same girl at all."

"So I noticed," Miss Ada said bluntly. "They have kipper this morning, George."

"Good. Are you feeling quite well, Cousin Ada? You look a bit liverish."

"I am not liverish. But I am concerned with the absurd activities of certain persons. It is a well-known fact that if one engages in violence, one ought to remain quiet thereafter." She gave George a penetrating scowl, but he did not appear to see any personal implication in her remark.

"I shall remember that, next time I engage in violence, Cousin Ada," he promised, smiling.

"That," she countered sharply, "was a distinctly American sort of remark and not worthy of you. I do wish you'd be careful."

"I am careful. I've always been careful. By the way, you no longer walk in your sleep, do you, dear?" He gave her a twinkling, amused look which was very irritating. Miss Ada stepped into the nearest elevator, reflecting that everyone seemed to have become contaminated with the American flippancy. Even George, who was always the soul of respectful manners where she was concerned. It was most disconcerting. "He'll be in the clink if he doesn't watch out," she said aloud.

The elevator boy said, "Ma'am?"

Walk in your sleep. What did he mean by that remark? Of course she didn't walk in her sleep. Hadn't done so for years. At least she didn't think she had.

Henry opened the studio and got out his brushes and paint for the interminable plaid job, and then Roscoe arrived. He had a bad head this morning, he said. Maybe he would get married, so he wouldn't have to spend his nights in bars. It was a lot of trouble to have to do that. Henry told him a wife was a lot of trouble too.

Roscoe rose to the bait. "You got the best wife in the world. Nobody like Miss Murdock. I give her my shirt any time." He was wearing one that would scarcely do for a respectable dog's bed, but Henry took this oath of allegiance in the spirit in which it was given. "You don't think she get mixed up with these phonies, Henry?"

"No. Emily never gets mixed up in anything." Henry was writing his answer to the ad in the *Times*. When it was finished he sent Roscoe out with it.

Fisher telephoned and asked facetiously about the pants, and Henry told him that Emily had taken them away from Marie Dennis.

"Mrs. Bryce encountered Marie? When?"

"Yesterday, about five o'clock, in Bloomingdale's. She's had her hair bleached."

"I don't suppose it occurred to you at the time that this information would have helped us to locate Marie?"

"To tell you the truth, we were busy. Somebody followed Emily home after she had these pants and knocked her out and cut off some of the buttons. Emily hadn't had a chance to see if there was something hidden in the buttons. During the evening our apartment and the suite occupied by our English friends at the Waldorf were both searched pretty thoroughly. Your work?"

"Not mine."

"Vittorio was having dinner at the Waldorf, and seemed to be waiting to see someone. Apparently he wants to talk to one of the Britishers, but they don't care to talk to him."

Fisher grunted. "I understand from a friend of yours in the Seventeenth Precinct, Bryce, that you were a little overactive in another murder a while back. I don't like to cut in on your entertainment, but I feel I ought to warn you that it isn't always safe to be friendly with people who slit their relatives' throats."

"You don't think it was Vittorio, then, who killed Palling?"

Fisher withdrew from that question, saying one couldn't be sure, but meanwhile it was a good idea to be careful.

"Is Lieutenant Burgreen helping you?" Henry asked.

"We can take care of our own knitting up here," Fisher snapped, and Henry knew it hadn't been a tactful question. He was also pretty sure that someone in the Seventeenth Precinct was working on the job. Probably they had a tail on the English people, in case one of them should lead to Marie Dennis.

"We haven't found anything to justify your suspicions about a smuggling deal," the sergeant went on in a more friendly tone. "Your crazy friend Vittorio yielded absolutely zero—made a thorough search of his country place and his studio. Routine agreement with Jerome, the London decorator, in regard to your work."

Henry didn't think they would put an agreement about smuggling into a letter. He wondered if Fisher would mind reading him the letter from Jerome.

"Don't see why I should," Fisher replied. "But I will." He turned from the phone and spoke to someone, and presently he cleared his throat and read:

> "*My dear Mr. Vittorio*:
> *This will confirm our arrangement with regard to the work to be done by your decorators for our Mr. George Peel in London. You are to send over to us Mr. and Mrs. Henry Bryce to finish two antique mahogany cabinets in a manner to be stipulated by me. You are to take full responsibility for the quality of the work.*
> *We agree to allow you in United States currency the sum of fifteen hundred dollars and you are to take care of Mr. and Mrs. Bryce. Any balance to be credited to the account in the Chase Bank, New York, of Mrs. Roy (Olivia) Palling, daughter of Mr. George Peel."*

"Would you mind reading that last sentence again?" Henry asked.

"Matter? Didn't you get your proper cut?" Fisher asked, and reread the sentence.

"Why should there be any balance?" Henry demanded. "And why should it be credited to Mrs. Palling rather than to Jerome? It sounds like a message to me."

"Thanks for your cooperation, Bryce," Fisher said. "I'll be in touch with you."

Henry wondered, after he had hung up, whether Fisher hadn't had the idea himself that this was a peculiar sentence. Perhaps he'd been trying Henry out. There was no reason to trust the Bryces more than anyone else who had been at Link's place the night of the murder.

Henry returned to his striping job, and then Emily arrived, brisk and eager for work, and wanted to know why he didn't have the chest finished and where Roscoe was. He evaded both questions, picked up the phone again, called Waterfall, got the barracks and Sergeant Fisher.

"I was just wondering," he said, "if Mrs. Palling has an account in the Chase Bank?"

Fisher coughed. "Odd you should think of that, Bryce. She has not."

"So you were just testing for termites when you read me that letter? May I ask if Vittorio has made any other arrangements for New York decorators to go to London?"

"As far as we know, he hasn't."

"I suppose you've been in touch with London and have the dope on Jerome?"

Fisher rejected that question by asking to speak to Mrs. Bryce if she was there now. He and Emily went into great detail then about Marie's new appearance.

Link came in, gleaming in a new suit and a new gray hat. He didn't go near anything, as most objects in the studio were either dusty or freshly painted.

"You do look beautiful, Link," Emily said. "But I hope you're armed. I wouldn't trust that pale, delicate female."

Link just smiled and said he would always remain true to Emily.

"Darling," Henry said, "do you know how much Vittorio was paid for your work in London? Fifteen hundred bucks."

Emily shrieked. "And all we got was a measly three hundred and expenses. That stinking Alfredo! Where are you taking Olivia to lunch, Link?"

The two of them discussed the merits of various eating houses, Emily focusing on the best clam dispensaries and Link considering dim lights and alcohol. With the aid of Emily's interference he decided on the Pierre. Henry considered telling Link about the sentence in Jerome's letter which mentioned Olivia, but decided not to. Let the poor dope be happy while he ate this momentous lunch. After lunch the hanging, maybe.

Link left the studio and went downstairs to his shop to kill time till half-past twelve, when Olivia was supposed to appear. A few minutes later Henry strolled down to see how Olivia was looking. At a quarter of one she hadn't arrived. Link grew more and more fidgety. Something horrible had happened to her, he was sure.

"My God," Henry said, "you've waited for women before. You know how they are. Maybe she's forgotten all about the date."

At one o'clock she came in, breathless and apologetic. "I'm most dreadfully sorry, Link," she said, looking really sorry. "It was something I had to do, and it took longer than I expected. I couldn't phone you. Will you forgive me?"

He did with a foolish grin, and took her off. After all the girls Link had worried into early spinsterhood, it was a pitiful sight to see him so utterly demented.

Henry gave some further thought to Olivia during lunch. He and Emily were eating in Joe's bar and grill, a dark, smelly place blessed with television and hard booths with black glass tables. If they didn't come in every so often Joe sent an emissary to see if they had been poisoned the last time.

He was thinking about Saturday night. Olivia ought to have noticed at some time during the night that her husband hadn't come to bed. At least it seemed so to Henry. And yet she had been the last to waken and come out in the morning when Emily found him dead.

"Now what are you hatching?" Emily demanded.

"If I didn't come home all night would you sleep peacefully until morning?"

"I'd have the police out, you know that."

"Of course you're not Olivia. Slight difference in temperament."

Emily blinked a couple of times, ate another mouthful of shrimp. "You mean why didn't Olivia get up to see where Roy was? She didn't like Roy."

"Makes it all the more likely that she would be aware of his absence, doesn't it?"

Emily agreed. "The more he didn't come the gladder she was. So she slept well."

"I don't think so. Curiosity would take her into the living room." He paused. "Maybe it did."

"I've thought right along she killed him, if that's all you mean. It takes you years to arrive at the simplest conclusions, Henry. We shouldn't have let her take Link out."

Henry observed that Link was doing the honors, and they couldn't have stopped him—he was sunk, murder or no murder. In fact, he wondered if Link wasn't rather attracted by the possibility that Olivia was guilty of cutting her husband's throat. A man didn't have dates like that every day.

"This is the day Miss Ada sells the Pennsylvania Railroad, isn't it?" Henry asked. "Perhaps she'll be along with a present for you, my pet. I think she likes you."

Emily looked pleased. "I think she does too. But she's awfully busy solving this murder—I doubt if she'll come to see us today." Emily's face fell open in surprise.

Turning, Henry saw a familiar tall, gaunt figure, topped with a hat of decided shape and bulk, carrying a knitting bag. Miss Birtwistle hesitated only momentarily at the entrance, advanced firmly to the bar, and stated in a clear voice, "I am looking for a Mr. Henry Bryce."

"Yes, ma'am," Joe said, and pointed. "He's right here."

Miss Ada came over, and Henry stood. "Your man informed me that you were here." She sat down. She had had her lunch, but she would take a ginger beer. Henry explained to Joe that this was not a combination of beer and ginger ale, and Miss Ada looked about her. "Rather like a tomb, isn't it?"

"You had no trouble getting your money from the broker?" Henry asked.

"None whatever. I deposited temporarily in the Chase Bank. Is it sound?"

"Fairly."

"I don't trust banks, and I detest bankers, but what is one to do with money? I kept a little out, in case of disaster." She took a dog-eared sealskin wallet from her knitting bag and Henry saw that it was stuffed with bills of no mean denomination.

"Put it away," Emily said fearfully. "People in New York are very fond of stuff like that. They could mug you."

Miss Ada took great interest in this new method of incapacitating a victim. "Americans are savage," she remarked. "I wonder if it could be the central heating. Excessive warmth makes one irritable, you know. An Englishman would never be warm enough to commit a murder except in midsummer. I'm worried about Cousin George," she added, changing the subject abruptly.

"Anything wrong?" Henry inquired.

"His health is good. But his spirits are drooping, and I'm afraid if they insist on detaining us much longer he will become quite restive. Always a poor traveler, George. He likes his home and his friends. I don't imagine there is anything one could do to hasten the processes of the law? One couldn't be allowed to return home on a sort of bond?"

Henry didn't know, but he offered to inquire for Miss Ada. Privately he thought there was no chance of any such release, and he wondered if Miss Ada were concerned for George Peel or for Olivia. Miss Ada was terribly fond of Olivia.

"I wouldn't try to leave, Miss Ada," Emily said, frowning. "It might look as if you were guilty. Anyway, you can have fun in New York. Think of all the newsreels."

Miss Ada spent most of the afternoon in the studio, sitting very straight on a chair that looked as if it might have carried Cleopatra down the Nile. It had once been what Emily politely called a commode. Miss Ada did not know this.

After a while George Peel dropped in, and Henry couldn't see any signs of restiveness or discontent in his pink and pleasant face. He had bought himself a couple of American pipes and some fancy tobacco at Dunhill's and he seemed once again rather pleased with life.

Link brought Olivia up after their protracted luncheon. She didn't listen to what was said to her, and she kept opening and closing the catch on her bag. Here, Henry thought, was the anxious member. Something decidedly on her mind. Miss Ada gave her a hundred dollars to spend and she left.

Emily was having her hair done at five, and this relieved Henry of explanations. Undoubtedly Emily would have enjoyed waiting behind the library to see who Uncle was, but Emily was too vocal to take to a tryst. He left a note in the apartment saying he had some business to attend to and would be late.

He had supper at a little restaurant in Sixty-fourth Street, strolled west to Fifth Avenue, and then down to Tiffany's corner, studied a very refined display of diamonds, and wished the prices were in the window. He wondered how many diamonds, of what dimensions, would be required to compose a fortune worth the risk of smuggling.

It was still early when he reached Forty-second Street, so he passed between the lions and up the steps, through the great lobby devoted to the inspection of briefcases which might conceal rare manuscripts, and down the hall to the wheezing elevator.

It was Henry's intention to study the diamond, but he found the encyclopedic treatment rather dull, except for a reference to the largest diamond in the world, owned by the Portuguese Government, who hadn't let anyone see it for more than a hundred years because they were afraid it was a topaz.

Henry returned the volumes to the old gentleman who kept things in order along the walls behind the little fence, and put in his order at the book cafeteria for a couple of things on Charles Edward Stuart. After a half-hour under a green-shaded lamp in the company of Charles's portraits and adventures, Henry concluded the prince had done rather well for a weak-faced fat young man with a dimple in his chin and a mother named Clementina. All the ladies were wild about him, which may have accounted for his changing his clothes so often on his flight. There was a reference to garments on display in Edinburgh Castle, donated by Colonel Bruno Birtwistle of Surrey.

Henry was delighted to find an illustration showing a pair of trousers almost the exact duplicate of those now in Emily's possession. He would have to bring her here and show it to her. There was also a note to the effect that in the left foot of this particular pair of trousers some thoughtful lady had made a secret pocket where Charles Edward could keep his change.

Miss Ada, with her pride in family history, doubtless knew about this little pocket. Had that given her an inspiration? But Miss Ada didn't need to smuggle—she had buckets of legitimate cash. At least he thought it was legitimate. But had anyone gone with Miss Ada this morning to the broker's? Perhaps her visit had been to some discreet, dark little shop which dealt in gems of questionable origin. The picture of Miss Ada dealing with a fence was so ridiculous that Henry laughed out loud, to the distress of a gentleman studying the action of wind in a tunnel.

He saw that it was almost nine, and he wanted to be at the meeting place before Uncle arrived. He left by the Forty-second Street door, walked round to the mall bordered with plane trees. It was quite dark now, and the lights of the park bloomed pale yellow in the soft air. Henry chose a bench, sat down to wait.

It seemed to grow more lonely in the dark as the minutes went by. The great back wall of the library shut one off from the city, the office buildings on Fortieth and Forty-second streets had only occasional lighted windows where some poor devil was figuring the square root of minus one or sloshing a mop about. He had chosen the place himself, for this very seclusion. No need to complain because it wasn't brightly lighted and swarming with people. He noticed a man sitting on one of the benches along the grass plot. He had his hat over his eyes and seemed to be sleeping. Poor bum, probably.

A figure appeared at the corner of the building on the Forty-second Street side, seemed to search the mall, didn't see him at first, then advanced with a familiar, determined step. Even in this light the height, the hat of character, and the knitting bag were easy to identify. Henry sat quite still, saw Miss Ada come toward him steadily, with no pause for surprise at the point where she must have recognized him.

"Hello, Uncle," he said, getting up.

"Good evening, Henry." Miss Ada smiled. "I rather thought you'd be here."

"You expected me?"

"Your grammar, my dear boy. One says, 'I shall be glad to meet you,' not 'I will.' "

Henry flushed. "So that was it. You received no answer from M.D., then?"

Miss Ada did not reply, but kept looking toward the corner where she herself had appeared. In a moment she rose. "There's no point in our hanging about like this, is there?" she asked. "Would you care for a ginger beer?"

"Sounds rather persuasive," Henry confessed. "There's a Schrafft's not far away. Very respectable." He automatically looked in the direction of Broadway and Forty-third Street, and saw the lone man get up and leave, rather quickly for a bum with no definite destination in mind. He looked at Miss Ada and knew that she had seen him, too, but there was no agitation in her voice as she said, "Where is Emily? I thought she was keen on this sort of thing?"

"Gave her the slip," Henry said. "That wasn't your Cousin George, was it?"

"Where?" Miss Ada looked all around blindly.

"Never mind. Couldn't have been, anyway." He took her arm and they made their way at a fairly brisk pace. As they came out of the open square at the Sixth Avenue end Henry glanced back, gave Miss Ada's arm an involuntary jerk.

"Now what's the matter?" she demanded, looking round.

"I think my mind is going. I thought I saw Olivia back there."

Miss Ada chuckled. "Why do they say 'nervous as an old woman'? It's the young who have nerves."

They found a table in the small cocktail room and Miss Ada immediately took out her wallet. "This is my treat," she said, and there was no dissuading her.

"I had some time to kill in the library just now," Henry told her. "I found out all about your great-uncle Bruno Birtwistle and the royal trousers in Edinburgh Castle."

Miss Ada's face changed, and not with pleasure. There was a distinct wariness in her shrewd gray eyes as she said, "And what did you learn that you didn't know before?"

"They had a secret pocket in the foot for carrying Charlie's traveler's checks."

"Really? I should think it might have been a trifle uncomfortable on a long walk. But perhaps Charles Edward was always on horseback."

Henry said he wondered if there had been such a pocket in the trousers Mr. Peel had given Emily.

"I've thought from the beginning they were merely a copy," Miss Ada stated firmly. "I doubt that anyone would go to the trouble of reproducing the pocket. And if someone had?"

"I still think Roy was trying to smuggle something into this country from England. Roy or someone else," he added thoughtfully, looking into his glass. "Perhaps the idea of using the trousers for that purpose would occur more readily to a person who knew about the pair in Edinburgh Castle with the secret pocket."

Miss Ada smiled slightly. "If one were engaged in smuggling one would scarcely need to learn tricks from a sentimental fool like Charles Edward."

Henry lifted a surprised eyebrow. He was sure Miss Ada wouldn't need to learn from anyone, but he hadn't expected her to refer to bankrupt royalty in this way. Perhaps she was more agitated than she appeared. "Think I'll go to bed early tonight," he said, yawning. "Haven't been sleeping too well."

Miss Ada, he could see, was glad the subject had been changed.

"Olivia," he continued in a bored voice, "is a wonderful sleeper. Imagine sleeping through the murder of one's husband. In the next room too."

"The poor child was exhausted," Miss Ada said, undisturbed by his insinuations.

Henry continued. "If she got up and looked at him during the night and saw that he was rendered harmless, perhaps she could sleep better. I believe she's too nervous a girl to be able to kill her husband and then have a good night's sleep."

Miss Ada was smiling at him now. "Bursting with theories, aren't you, Henry?"

He rather liked her to call him Henry. He was beginning to feel he had known Miss Ada all his life. When she took up her bulging wallet to pay the check, he said, "Miss Ada, have you always carried your money in a knitting bag?"

"No. I feel it looks less tempting to one of your muggers than a handbag."

Perhaps she was right. He took her to the hotel and up to their rooms, where Olivia and Mr. Peel were waiting. They both seemed excessively glad to see their cousin and grateful to Henry for delivering her.

"We were worried," Olivia said, smiling a little. "One never knows what Cousin Ada will do."

"When one knows exactly what one will do, and everyone else knows what one will do," Miss Ada pronounced, "one had better be dead. Marie did not answer my advertisement."

Mr. Peel looked startled. "You advertised for Marie?"

"One must try everything. The girl is an absolute nitwit, but I believe she has information which would be helpful in finding Roy's murderer. And then, too, she's probably frightened half to death and would be glad if we found her. I shouldn't like to be 'hiding out,' as they call it here, should you?"

"No, I shouldn't," Mr. Peel agreed, "particularly with my hair bleached." He went over and inspected himself in a mirror.

"I suppose one has one's eyebrows done to match?"

Henry refused a drink, went down to the street, and found a cab. "Grand Central," he said, and had barely time to be nervous about the speed down Park Avenue before they arrived. He bought a ticket to Waterfall, and had four minutes to catch the only train in the next two hours.

If he'd thought, he might have asked Link to come along, but there wasn't time now and he could get into the house with the key which hung on the garage. It would have been a little more cheery with Link, but he felt confident there was no danger in the expedition. The three people he favored as possible murderers were all on their way to bed in the Waldorf, not in the least aware of his journey.

He was going back to Link's house because he had thought of an explanation for Olivia's not hearing anything and not noticing that Roy hadn't come to bed. "Oblivious Olivia," he said to himself as the smoky old cars rattled through 125th Street. "I'd be willing to bet she wakes up on an average of twenty times during the night. She's the tossing-and-turning type."

Up near Tarrytown he got to thinking about Roy. If Emily were right and Roy had gone through her dressing case, and if Roy had also told Marie to go to the studio and take Charlie's pants, then Roy had not been the smuggler. The smuggler would know exactly where the loot was hidden, and wouldn't try first Emily's luggage and then Charlie's pants. Unless someone had found him out and moved the loot. That was possible, of course. In that case, perhaps what they were looking for was still in Link's house.

The idea made him perspire slightly. Lucky he hadn't mentioned his trip to the three at the hotel, just in case one of them had a nice little cache up here.

Another possibility occurred to him. Roy had found his illegal importation without any trouble, had hidden it somewhere on Link's place, had then called Marie and told her to steal the trousers as a red herring. Perhaps he had also told her where the stuff was. Perhaps not. Miss Ada said Marie was stupid, but Miss Ada saw a heavy cloud of stupidity overhanging the human race. "Perhaps she tells other people I'm stupid," Henry thought. "I'll bet she does. Maybe she's right. Maybe I'm a damned fool to come up here alone."

Mr. Beaman's taxi was parked at the station in Waterfall, and Henry got into it. Beaman remembered him.

"You were here over the weekend," he said, passing a vegetable truck.

"I was," Henry admitted. "Any news about the murder?"

Beaman shook his head. "I was talking to Fisher this evening about suppertime, and he said they don't know any more than they did when they started. But Fisher always talks that way till he's absolutely sure. He can't stand bein' wrong, you know."

"You don't have much crime up here, do you?" Henry inquired, watching the road.

"Few housebreakings during the winter, mostly crazy kids lookin' for excitement. Haven't had a murder in years."

"You can let me off at the top of the drive," Henry told him.

"Okay. But it's no trouble to run down to the house and turn around."

"Thanks, but I'd rather you didn't."

Beaman grinned. "You want to sneak up on him, eh? Why do you think they brought that Englishman over here to bump him off?" He slowed, pulled into the clover, and stopped.

Henry didn't know.

"I guess it's the regulations," Beaman concluded. "You can't do anything under these socialist governments."

Henry got out, and Beaman said to give him a ring when he wanted to go back to town.

Henry was always surprised at the darkness of a clear night in the country. The stars were sharp in the sky but the roadway under his feet was black. He moved along carefully in the loose gravel, making his way down the slope and then to the right toward the garage. He reached up to the nail under the eaves. The key was there. Damned-fool place to keep a key, he had told Link. Anybody could break into the house. Link kept some tempting things here, too—the toaster and the radios and the liquor, if you didn't happen to need furniture.

He argued with Link in his mind as he turned toward the house, his eyes growing accustomed to the dark now, so that he could make out the pattern of the gardens, then the pale pansies glimmering in the bed under the living-room windows, then the shiny knob on the kitchen door.

As he came closer the door seemed to be slightly open, but of course it couldn't be—he had watched Link lock it on Monday morning as they left.

He stopped. It was open. He waited, listening all round him. Nothing stirred. There was no sound from inside the house. He tried to thaw his frozen muscles by telling himself a professional housebreaker had been through and left the door open after he took what he wanted.

Or perhaps the gardener had been over. He knew where Link kept the key. But would the gardener have left the house open and replaced the key on its hook?

Henry ventured a step forward, but the sound of his feet in the gravel seemed deafening. He listened again. No one moved. He cleared his throat, called huskily, "Who's here?"

No response. Well, he told himself, he couldn't stand here shivering all night. Either there was somebody in there or there wasn't, and he'd better find out. Of course he could go back to town and get Fisher. But it was a long walk, and by that time they'd be gone.

"I wish I were brave," he said to himself, inching toward the doorway and stepping cautiously through it into the kitchen. He stopped once more to see if his approach had caused any alarm inside, and he could feel perspiration trickling down his thighs.

There was a sound. It was so ludicrous he didn't believe it at first. Someone was snoring. In the living room. Henry stepped quietly onto the carpet, trying to see without a light.

The snores came from the big chair beside the fireplace, the one Roy had been sitting in when he was murdered. Henry moved toward the chair, bumped something. There was a crash, and he stood still, gritting his teeth and waiting for the sleeper to spring toward him.

The sleeper went right on sleeping. It must be a trap. Nobody could sleep through that noise even in his own bed. And here was this person in a strange house, probably stealing, with every reason to be alert. Curiosity began to conquer Henry's fear. He lighted a lamp.

Sitting up with great dignity, except for an open mouth, was a short, square man with a sandy beard, wearing a derby, a brown suit with trousers that came up to his armpits, an unbuttoned vest, a white shirt, a black tie, a pair of brown gloves, and a serene expression. Leaning against his knee was a furled black umbrella.

On the table at his side were a glass and a bottle. Leaning closer, Henry saw that it looked like the bottle of madeira Alfredo had given them for Olivia.

The light disturbed the man. His eyelids fluttered, sprang open, revealing two little blue buttons which regarded Henry with amazement. "I say, who are you?" he demanded.

"I say, who are you?" Henry countered.

He blinked slowly, took it square, and explained, "Mr. Simpson promised to meet me here. I've waited ever so long. Must have dozed a bit."

"Dozed?" Henry said. "You were dead to the world. You know Mr. Simpson?"

"Only slightly. My name, by the way, is Hedges. I buy antiques in a modest way."

Henry nodded, sat down opposite Mr. Hedges. He certainly didn't look like an antique dealer, but then he was English.

"Have any trouble getting in?" Henry asked politely.

"No, oh no. Simpson was good enough to give me a key. What time is it?" Henry told him. "Oh, dear. I shan't wait any longer. Something obviously has made it impossible for Mr. Simpson to keep the appointment. How does one return to town?"

"How did you come?"

"Cab. But I didn't ask him to wait, believing Mr. Simpson would arrange the return himself."

It was a good story, Henry reflected, and if it wasn't true he told it awfully well. His manner was not too easy. It was a deft combination of dignity and embarrassment, suitable to a man caught in someone's else house at an odd time of night, but with a legitimate excuse.

"You planned to return to New York?" Henry asked.

Mr. Hedges nodded, regarding Henry with a hopeful and trusting expression while he buttoned his vest.

Henry considered the situation for a moment. He couldn't do

what he had planned with Mr. Hedges present. Perhaps if he accompanied him to New York he would discover whether the story was a fabrication, and, if so, who Hedges really was.

"I'll order a cab for us," he said, making up his mind.

"That's very good of you. Did you mention your name?"

"Old friend of Simpson's," Henry answered, going to the phone in the hall.

While they waited for Beaman's taxi, Henry went back to the bedrooms, on the pretext of personal business. As far as he could see, nothing had been disturbed. At any rate, there was no evidence of a clumsy or hasty search.

On the train Mr. Hedges chatted pleasantly about the difficulty of finding nice old pieces at a price one wished to pay, mentioned the nuisances connected with the skillful manufacture of new antiques, and as they pulled into Grand Central Henry realized that he had said exactly nothing.

"I shall phone Mr. Simpson from here, I think," Hedges said as they entered the station on the lower level.

"He lives in our block," Henry told him. "If you're going over to see him, we may as well save cabfare and go together."

"Fine." Hedges smiled, hurrying away toward a row of phone booths.

That was the last Henry saw of him. How he got out of the booth and away, Henry never knew.

As soon as he realized he had been ditched he made for Link's apartment in Sixty-second Street.

"You look like an old baked bean," Link greeted him cordially. "Sit down and take the pallor off your face."

"I've just been up to your place in the country," Henry began, and told him the story.

Link chuckled. "You actually think you saw this little man in a derby asleep by the fireplace?"

"Of course I saw him. We came into New York together. He had a terribly British accent."

Link shook his head. "Better lay off that stuff, my boy."

"You don't know anybody by the name of Hedges who buys antiques?"

"No. And I don't believe there is anybody named Hedges who

buys antiques." Link poured him a highball, remarking that he might as well be drunk.

"Then who the devil is he?" Henry wondered. "What was he after in your house? If he's British, and he obviously is, then he may have some connection with our friends. Link!" He slapped the table. "Maybe he killed Roy!"

"You'll have a hot chance of convincing Fisher. Who ever heard of a murderer who returned to take a nap at the scene of the crime? And from what you say, he was sitting in the very spot where Roy was murdered. No, I'm afraid that doesn't tie."

"I still don't see how he got away from me," Henry muttered. "I was right there all the time. Maybe he didn't go into the phone booth at all."

Link observed that the man was either a figment of Henry's imagination or a very clever fellow indeed. "He made you believe that he had a perfect right to be in my house alone. He told you absolutely nothing, you say, in that long ride from Waterfall to the city. And then he ditched you as easily as if you'd been a two-year-old."

"And he didn't even look very bright," Henry added dismally.

"Professional housebreaker," Link remarked.

"He wouldn't risk falling asleep on a job, would he?"

"You said he'd had a drink."

"He was only drinking wine. He had the bottle Alfredo gave us for Olivia." Henry paused. This was the explanation he'd been looking for. "Link," he said, "do you remember how Olivia acted the morning of the murder? Sort of dopey? She didn't wake up when Emily found the body, and fell down and all that. And yet Olivia's room was next to the living room."

Link sat up. "You think Olivia was drugged, by means of the wine?"

"Doesn't it seem possible?"

"If she was, that sort of lets her out as a murderer, doesn't it?" Link was looking very happy.

"It certainly does. Unless she put a shot of something in the bottle herself, and acted drugged."

Link stopped smiling. "You're a friend. She wouldn't do a thing like that. Not Olivia."

"You don't know Olivia. Seems to me she's pretty gay for a widow of three days. I wouldn't trust the wench."

"Who wouldn't be gay after she got rid of a rat like Palling? Anyway, I don't consider going out to lunch with me an indiscretion."

Henry said that depended on one's point of view. He added that he was only kidding, and he himself didn't believe Olivia was guilty of murder. He would call Fisher in the morning about the little man in the derby and about the wine. If Alfredo had drugged the bottle before he gave it to them, that put a new light on his part in the drama.

"By the way," Link said, "you didn't happen to mention why you went up to Waterfall."

"I wanted to find out it Olivia had been drugged—and it seems I did. Also, I had an idea the smuggled items—whatever they are—might still be in your house. They haven't turned up anywhere else, so I thought maybe I could find them up there."

Link pointed out that Fisher and his men had done a thorough job on the house.

"Maybe the stuff wasn't hidden in the house. Maybe it was buried, or stuck in a tree or something."

"It would have been clever to drop it into the pool, once Fisher had finished draining it and prodding around the muck, and filled it up again."

"Where was it in the meantime?"

"Oh, in a box of Kleenex or wrapped up in a waffle." Link leaned back, stretched his long, thin legs, and yawned. "I bet they find it in a very simple, obvious place, right under their noses."

"Let's go back up to Waterfall tomorrow and look around," Henry suggested.

"How will you get away? I understand you have a very urgent plaid job for old lady Cormorant."

"I'll think of an excuse."

He found Emily pacing the floor in their apartment while Hilda Leghorn pleasantly suggested a variety of horrible accidents. "He's probably in the morgue right now," she was saying as Henry came in.

"Not yet, dear," he answered. "How's the oil business?"

"Henry!" Emily cried. "I called all the bars!"

Hilda leaned back on the sofa, prepared to enjoy a scene.

"Awfully nice of you to come over to help Emily worry," Henry told her. "See you tomorrow." He held the door open.

"Where were you?" Emily asked, as soon as Hilda had plunked down the stairs.

"I'll tell you all about it," he promised. "Make me one of your terrible fried-egg sandwiches, will you?"

Emily, flattered by this request, rushed to the kitchen and clattered around while Henry told her about his meeting behind the library with Miss Ada, and his encounter with the short, square man with the sandy beard up at Link's place. By the time he had finished, Emily had created a welter of eggshells, broken dishes, and burnt matches.

"Here it is," she said, triumphantly handing him a mound on a plate. "You know what I think? Miss Ada followed you to Waterfall, made a mad dash to Link's house, and was sitting in front of the fireplace in a derby when you got there."

"That's very good deduction, dear. What's in this besides Worcestershire?"

"No kidding," Emily said, frowning, "Miss Ada turns up pretty often in rather funny places, don't you think?"

He nodded, chewing.

"She drugged Olivia so Olivia wouldn't wake up and catch her cutting up Roy. But I can't think of Miss Ada as a murderess. Or Mr. Peel either. He's so cute you could put a gold chain on him and keep him for a pet. He affects me just like a little old Sealyham."

"If I didn't dream that little man in the derby," Henry said suddenly, "maybe he's the fellow who sat on our sofa last night and drank our brandy."

Emily looked startled. "Yes. He drinks wherever he works. But what is his work?"

"Searching houses, apparently. Didn't Mr. Peel say that the whiskey bottle in their sitting room had been moved while we were all at dinner last night?"

Emily sighed. "It gets foggier and foggier as far as I'm concerned."

Henry, exhausted, let go of the whole problem, undressed, and fell into bed.

"Henry," Emily said, "you ought to be nicer to Hilda."

"Why?"

"She's going to be filthy rich."

"I suppose I'm to ask how."

"She's in the nose-oil business."

Henry thought he hadn't really heard.

"Have you ever noticed that people's noses don't wrinkle?"

"Not particularly. Have you?"

"I mean when they get old, their noses stay young."

Henry said not if they drank. Emily brushed this aside. "Hilda and some big man in the beauty business are going to sell nose oil instead of cold cream, for keeping your skin young."

Henry made a derisive noise and turned over.

Chapter 8

Sergeant Fisher, when Henry called him in the morning, showed very little interest in the story about the man in the derby. He brushed it aside in favor of the meeting with Miss Ada in Bryant Park. That seemed to appeal to him. Perhaps he thought Henry had been drinking.

Henry worked conscientiously until ten o'clock, then Olivia and her father and Miss Ada came in, on their way to a tour of the city. Miss Ada felt they should put in some of their time profitably, and she especially wanted to see the Stock Exchange. She planned to have lunch at a safe distance while Olivia did the Metropolitan and Mr. Peel met the men at the Central Park Zoo. Mr. Peel was keen on zoos.

They were leaving when Link came up, and Olivia wanted him to join the party, but Link refused, regretfully.

A few minutes later Link and Henry went out for coffee, leaving Roscoe and Emily in the studio.

"Have you thought of an excuse?" Link asked, as they dropped onto stools in the drugstore.

Henry said he thought it would be better just to leave, and give the excuses when he came back. Emily was pretty shrewd about some things. So they turned the key in Link's shop and hailed a cab. As he got in, Henry saw the nose-oil queen spying from the doorway of her beauty salon across the street.

When they reached Waterfall they took Beaman's cab and stopped off at the barracks to see Fisher. He didn't seem particularly elated by the visit.

"We wondered if you'd heard anything about Marie Dennis?" Link asked agreeably, offering him a cigarette.

"She's been questioned. No help there."

"You found her, then," Henry said.

"Naturally."

"And she didn't know a thing about Palling's death or any smuggling deal?"

Fisher shook his head. "She broke down and admitted she came over because of Palling—afraid something might happen to him. She phoned him Saturday and then he called her back and told her to remove a pair of trousers from your studio as soon as it opened on Monday morning. She didn't know there was anything valuable concealed in the trousers."

"Why did she think he wanted them?" Link demanded.

"You ought to have done the questioning, Mr. Simpson."

Henry wanted to know if Marie was in jail.

"On what charge?" Fisher countered. "She asked for the pants and your man gave them to her. Anyway, we'd rather have her at liberty. She may give us a lead. She's living in a furnished room on Fiftieth Street, off Third Avenue, for your information." He leaned back in his chair and regarded them unfavorably. "What's your mission up here?"

Henry explained that they wanted to look more thoroughly for something which might have been smuggled in from England.

"The jewels or the papers?" Fisher inquired acidly.

"People do occasionally bring things in," Link insisted. "If they don't, what are all those men doing in customs? We thought maybe they threw the stuff into the pool after you'd drained it, instead of before."

Fisher looked surprised. "Let me know if the bottom is lined with emeralds," he said, but he was interested all the same.

They went on, and when they reached the cottage Link got a shovel and a pick and a crowbar and they set to diverting the stream around the swimming pool again, but this time it wasn't such a job as the ditch had been dug by Fisher's men on Sunday. Then they trudged around on the bottom, examining every heap of leaves, looking under every twig and stone. If there was something hidden there, they reasoned, it would be protected by a tin box or at least a handkerchief.

Finally Link wiped his face with his sleeve and said he was satisfied. "Nice exercise. Shall we see if there's anything left from Sunday in the icebox?"

They found a chicken wing and a dry waffle, which they divided between them. Then Henry wondered if the stream above or below the pool could have been used as a hiding place, and they went outside again and waded up and down in the icy, swift water, their toes turning blue and their noses running.

"Seems to me Fisher takes his job pretty casually," Link observed, detaching his trouser cuff from a snag. "It's nice to rest your rear on a rubber cushion in a heated office while murderers gallop around the country."

"We're doing his work. You saw him prick up his ears when I mentioned the pool. Let's give this up and do a job on the garage and the rock garden, and then call it a day."

Link agreed. They also went over the house again, but all their work produced no larger results than the discovery of a bottle of Canadian Club Link had considered dead months ago. The madeira bottle was still on the table by the fireplace, almost empty. They took that and left it with Fisher on their way to the train.

When Henry reached the studio at four o'clock Roscoe was alone.

"Miss Murdock got a call from Emery. She's gone about an hour. Lucky for you."

"Lucky?" Henry repeated.

"Plenty sore at you, Bryce. 'Where's that man? Who does he think he is, going off in the middle of the day without no message?' I tell her I can finish up that chest for you, but she say shut up and do your own work, Roscoe, so I say okay." Roscoe grinned. "You find out something, Bryce?"

Henry shook his head. "Not a thing, Roscoe. And I missed lunch. Go out and get me a sandwich and a cup of coffee, will you?"

Roscoe was always glad to go on errands, and while he was out Henry changed his clothes and set to work on the plaid job.

It was exacting work. You needed a steady hand and a good head. Henry made swift progress at first, then he began to have trouble keeping his striping brush on the line. He held his hand out in front of him. It trembled. His head felt a little fuzzy, too, and there was an uneasiness in his stomach.

"Where'd you get that sandwich, Roscoe?" he demanded.

"Gottlieb's, like always. Whatsamatter? You don't look so good, Bryce."

"I don't feel so good, either. Call up Gottlieb for me."

Roscoe laid down the rag with which he had been rubbing a Japanese lacquer coffee table and went about the complex business of dialing the phone. Gottlieb came on and Henry asked him if he'd served any of that roast beef to other people.

"Sure, all day, Mr. Bryce. What gives? Something is wrong?"

"I feel very sick, Gottlieb, and I was in excellent health before I ate that sandwich. What about the coffee?"

Gottlieb was offended. He never poisoned his customers, not even Miss Leghorn, who deserved it. "You drink a little too much and you say poor Gottlieb is poison you. I am surprise, Mr. Bryce. I am surprise." His voice was developing tears of self-pity.

"I haven't had a drink today," Henry snapped irritably. "But forget the whole thing. Maybe I caught cold." He hung up abruptly and made for the washroom at the rear of the studio. He was sick and then he felt sleepy. Roscoe hung over him anxiously, breathing garlic and giving out diagnoses of everything from black plague to mumps.

"I heard about a man going to the hospital with the mumps," he said cheerfully. "It makes a man good and sick."

"I haven't got mumps," Henry groaned, clearing a couple of chairs off an Empire sofa with threadbare pink satin upholstery and lying down on it. "I'm just sick, that's all."

Roscoe felt his forehead. "You're cold," he said. "Also you look blue. This is not good, I think. I call the doctor?"

"No. I'll be all right." Henry closed his eyes and blue lights swam around in his head. He opened them again and saw that Roscoe seemed to be in some sort of deep spiritual struggle. He was looking down at Henry and blinking.

"I gotta ask you something, Bryce," he said abruptly, making up his mind. "You dye your hair?"

"What?" Henry snorted and closed his eyes again.

"You can tell me. Because I know how it is. I gotta friend puts dye on his head."

It was well known to Emily and Henry that Roscoe had been dyeing his hair for the last ten years, in order to make better headway with the girls, but Roscoe didn't think anybody knew. Henry said he would rather hear about this friend who colored his hair some other time. Right now he didn't feel keenly interested.

"I gotta reason to bring it up," Roscoe insisted. "Once this fellah gets hold of some very bad stuff. He don't know it, but the stuff could kill him. Anna Line, they call it. He turns blue. He gets cold and he is sick like you. I don't tell nobody if you been putting stuff on your hair."

Henry opened an eye. "What saved your friend?"

"I give him transfusion of whiskey."

"Let's try it. My wallet's in my other pants."

"I got money," Roscoe said haughtily, and hurried away.

Henry lay there, growing more and more drowsy, not caring whether Roscoe ever came back. Everything was far away and unimportant as he floated on pink satin.

Roscoe returned, breathless, nervously unscrewed the cap, and applied the bottle to Henry's lips. Henry very nearly drowned, but presently he began to feel warmer.

"You gonna be all right," Roscoe said anxiously, putting his ear down on Henry's chest. "Heart still going. I think you don't die."

"Fine," Henry said. "Maybe I'd better have another drink."

He was taking it when Emily came in, done up in her black dress and pearls and mink jacket, a costume she assumed as armor against decorators who liked to oppress the poor.

She didn't have to study the scene—it spoke. "Don't mind me," she said. "I only work here."

"Bryce is very sick," Roscoe told her seriously. "He damn near dies."

"Oh yes?" Emily stalked to the washroom and took off her good clothes. "He didn't kill himself working, did he?" The metal hangers rattled as she seized her jeans and hung up her dress. "Now I've got to finish that chest or be a burnt offering in the morning."

"You hate striping. I'll do it," Henry insisted, sitting up and trying the floor. It was going by in humps.

Emily reappeared, buttoning her shirt. "You may as well sleep it off, Henry. But I wish you'd get drunk on weekends."

"He is sick, I'm telling you, Miss Murdock," Roscoe pleaded. "He eats bad meat from Mr. Gottlieb and it comes right up." He winked at Henry, touched his scalp.

Emily was scornful. Gottlieb had never poisoned anybody and

never would. "Where's your brush?" she demanded, rooting through the cans and sticks and brushes on the table by the window.

Henry didn't remember where he had laid it down, he'd been in rather a hurry. He made his way unsteadily toward her, looking here and there for the striping brush.

"Oh, go and lie down," Emily said impatiently. "You're only getting in the way." She sniffed. "What smells so funny? It's you, Henry."

"Don't malign good whiskey, dear."

"It isn't whiskey. Roscoe, don't you smell anything?"

"Yeah." Roscoe went over to the can of paint Henry had been using and held it to his nose. "It comes from here."

Emily agreed. "Something very strange here, Sherlock," she said. "Did you swallow some of the paint?"

Henry found the brush he had been using, and it had an even stronger odor. None of them knew what it was.

"You got bumps on your hand," Roscoe noticed, pointing to Henry's right hand.

Henry saw that there was an eruption along his thumb and first and second fingers. He dropped the brush. "Don't anybody touch this," he said. "There's something on the handle."

Emily became a tornado of worry and action. She called Dr. Quinlan. She asked Henry every three minutes how he felt now. She sent Roscoe out for black coffee. She phoned Hilda and told her Henry was probably dying of some weird South American arrow poison, so Hilda came over to enjoy the death pangs. Henry thought it was easier to bear Emily's disapproval than her sympathy.

Henry was feeling a little better by the time Dr. Quinlan arrived. Quinlan took his pulse, sniffed at him, looked at his hand, said, "Harumph" a couple of times, and wanted to know if they used aniline oil in their paint mixtures. They did not. Was this a new type of pigment? It wasn't—they'd bought their supplies from the same reliable old firm for years, and nothing like this had ever happened. In fact, Henry had worked all morning with the same materials, with no ill effects.

"You think it's aniline?" Henry asked.

"Symptoms might possibly indicate it," Quinlan admitted cautiously. "But mere external contact shouldn't have such severe effects. Were you eating anything while you painted?"

"I had a sandwich and coffee."

"Umm." Quinlan's white eyebrows showed his gratification. "The oil undoubtedly was on your hand and was transferred to the bread which you ate."

"Yes, but how did the oil get on my brush in the first place?" Henry demanded.

"I'm a doctor," Quinlan reminded him, writing a beautiful illegible prescription.

"Your wonderful English friends have been planting poison around the studio," Hilda suggested, looking pleased. "I wonder what else they've left? You might go back to the washroom and set off a bomb. Or there might be a gun with a trigger all wired up in one of these chairs." She waved at the furniture piled on both sides of the aisle to the back of the studio. "Anything could be hidden in here and you wouldn't find it for months, and then all of a sudden, bang!"

"Or you might come over someday and sit on the thing and bang," Henry added.

The doctor said Henry would probably be all right in a day or two, although coffee would have been a better treatment than whiskey, collected his fee, and departed.

"I was sure right," Roscoe said. "You got Anna Line."

"You're as good a doctor as Quinlan," Henry told him. "And a lot cheaper. Let's close up."

"A funny thing," Roscoe observed, scratching his scalp. "Vittorio don't get sick when he picks up this brush."

"What did you say?" Emily demanded. "Was Alfredo here?"

"Sure. He talks to me a long time while I work."

"And he messed around with this brush and paint?" Henry asked.

"You know how he does—sticks his nose in the cans, picks up this and picks up that, and asks what is it, who wants it, and all that." Roscoe was frowning. "You think Vittorio done dirty work here?"

Henry shrugged. "Who knows? Let's go home."

Hilda wanted to hang around and chew the fat over who had

done this dastardly deed to Henry, but they got her out and went home. Emily called up Link, who came over immediately.

He showed proper concern over Henry's indisposition. "You know," he said thoughtfully, "Alfredo would be equal to this sort of thing. Knows about aniline, probably."

"Maybe. But why? I haven't done anything to Alfredo, aside from hating his guts."

"You could tell if he did it," Emily said thoughtfully.

"How?"

"If he has bumps on his hand, he didn't do it. He'd be careful."

Henry and Link looked at her admiringly. "Brains, that's what the little woman has."

"I'll go and see him," Link decided immediately. "Then we'll know."

Harry wanted to go along, but they wouldn't let him. It took Link a half-hour to make the trip to Alfredo's studio and back. Alfredo was not there.

"So we have four possibilities," Henry reflected. "Miss Ada, Mr. Peel, Olivia, and Alfredo."

"Let's not include Olivia in anything like this," Link objected.

"Why not?" Henry demanded. "She was here this morning with her father and Miss Ada. They all milled around for a half-hour. No one was watching them with the idea that they might drop nasty stuff on paintbrush handles. I was at the phone a couple of times with my back to the paint cans. And they all saw that that was my brush. But if they wanted to kill me," he added, puzzled, "why use such a clumsy method?"

"They didn't intend to kill you," Link suggested. "They wanted to make you sick. And succeeded."

"So you wouldn't be able to think about the murder," Emily added. "They're afraid you might solve it, Henry. Isn't that flattering?"

"Terribly. I wish I were as clever as they seem to think I am. Know what? I'm going to make a call at the Waldorf."

"You are not," Emily said. "What for?"

"See how they smell."

Link laughed and said he wouldn't be able to detect odors, he smelled so strongly of aniline himself.

"I might scare 'em if I went sniffing around the premises," Henry insisted.

"You're tight," Emily said. "Lie down."

He still thought it was a good idea, but he knew that Old Crow was apt to give a glossy appearance to inferior projects, so he lay down.

Link went home, and Emily, too tired even to read gore, fell into bed and slept. Henry, in a state of semiconsciousness, listened to the clock ticking and the slap of the Venetian blind as the breeze waved it in and out against the window frame. His mind went on knitting the yarn of murder, but it was the sort of work a child would do, full of knots and big and little stitches. One ought to rip it all out and start from the beginning again, back in the Royal Rajah. The night Emily's shoes had been crudely unnailed. Miss Ada coming along the hall from the bathroom, very softly. In the morning the package containing the epaulets outside the door. The sudden desire of the whole family and Marie Dennis to go to the United States. The plane trip. Mr. Peel dozing peacefully, after a pipe or two. Olivia and Roy quarreling in subdued, almost inaudible voices. Miss Ada taking an interest in everything. Asking questions of the hostess. Having a blanket wrapped round her knees. Marching back to the washroom, erect, defying the plane to drop into a pocket while she was in transit.

He chuckled at the memory of Miss Ada peering into the little containers of food and drink placed on her lap by the stewardess.

"Ye gods," he said suddenly, and sat up. Miss Ada had taken Emily's dressing case into the ladies' room! She had stayed there a very long time. So long that Henry remembered wondering if she were ill.

He looked at his watch. Nearly twelve. Couldn't do it now. Have to figure out something in the morning. He was so excited at having placed one piece of the puzzle in its proper slot that he didn't pay much attention, at first, to the implications. When he did, he felt sad.

In the morning Emily, with a tremendous effort of will, got up first, and made some foul coffee. She brought it to Henry's bed in one of the Dresden cups and sat down to watch him drink it. "Are you sure you feel better? You're not just faking so I won't worry?"

"No. If I don't suffer a relapse from this coffee I think I'll pull through."

"You'd better rest today, Henry. Stay in bed."

"What about Mrs. Cormorant's chest?"

Emily said she could wait for her old chest. "I'll fry you some eggs, Henry."

"If you don't mind, I'll fix my own. You run along, dear."

Emily looked hurt, then comforted herself. "I'd rather eat at Gottlieb's anyway." After six more inquiries on his physical state she finally left, and Henry called Fisher in Waterfall. The madeira, Fisher said, contained traces of phenobarbital.

Henry dressed, made some decent coffee, and rode down to Alfredo's studio.

Alfredo was there. So was Link Simpson.

"He has the lucky blisters," Link said at once. "But he wasn't sick."

Henry wanted to see the blisters, and Alfredo was happy to show them. "I saw them this morning when I washed," he said, contemplating his fingers. "You were sick, Bryce?"

"Yes. I ate some of the stuff, Doc Quinlan thought. Came off my hands on a sandwich. Of course," Henry said, turning to Link, "a smart fellow putting aniline into somebody's paint pot would get a bit on himself. Looks better, don't you think?"

"What do you mean?" Vittorio bristled. "I don't know about this aniline business. I have nothing against you."

"No? Maybe you think I'm too curious about a certain bloody event of last Saturday night."

Alfredo swelled up and got red all over. "I had nothing to do with it, and you know it. If they had something on me they'd lock me up, wouldn't they?"

"Sure," Link agreed; "he's just a poor, innocent smuggler. Let the guy alone, Henry."

Vittorio took a deep breath, expelled it with a whistling sound, then abruptly liquefied in a smile. Henry didn't believe the fellow had any real feelings; he struck various attitudes to see what effect they had on his audience. It was as easy for him as changing a tie.

"You don't seem to be having a nervous breakdown this morning, Alfredo," Henry remarked pleasantly. "Quick recovery, wasn't it?"

"I do that," Vittorio explained. "I go all to pieces. But I snap back." His little eyes glinted slyly. "The police don't tell you everything, do they?"

"What gives you that peculiar impression?" Link asked.

"I gave them some angles yesterday. They know I didn't kill Palling."

"The angles involved someone else, I take it." Henry studied Alfredo's smooth, fat front. "Who?"

"Mrs. Palling."

"You're a liar," Link said fiercely. "You'd do anything to save your own dirty skin."

Alfredo examined his pink hands complacently. "Two showers a day and a manicure twice a week. Your Mrs. Palling is a woman of judgment. Very wise in these times to have money in an American bank." He paused. "But her ideas about murder are rather naive. If I were deleting one husband I should certainly try to make it look like someone else's work. Or possibly suicide."

"What makes you think she did it?" Henry asked.

Vittorio shrugged. "I'm doing a job for Mrs. Stokowski. Might use Emily. Interested?"

"No," Henry said rudely. "Your jobs have too many strange angles. And you make the profit. Slight difference between fifteen hundred and three hundred."

Alfredo had enough blood left in his flexible conscience to cause a faint pink to rise to his forehead. "I was going to make that up to you and Emily," he said. "Really, Henry."

"Oh, sure." Henry and Link tried a few more questions, but the answers Vittorio gave were so unsatisfactory that they gave up and left him.

Link looked at his watch as they stood outside in the courtyard. "I've got to open the shop. Where are you going, Henry?"

"I have a little business at the Waldorf. Emily thinks I'm in bed, so don't give me away."

"Okay. Sure you feel up to poking your nose in?"

"Nothing more bracing, as Miss Ada would say, than a bit of Sherlock Holmes." As he mentioned her name he had a twinge of sadness. Oh well, one had to follow the threads no matter where they led.

Link said he thought he would phone Olivia and tell her what Alfredo had said.

"Go ahead," Henry agreed. "Gives you an excuse to talk to her, if you need one." He walked across Forty-eighth Street to the hotel and used a house phone. There was no answer from the suite, so he decided to leave a note for Miss Ada. He was at the mail desk when Mr. Peel came along.

"Good morning, Bryce," Peel said heartily. "Looking for us?"

"I really wanted to see Miss Birtwistle," Henry told him.

"I had breakfast with her. Now where did she say she was off to this morning? Seems to me it was the Stock Exchange. Place fascinates the old girl. Nothing I could do for you, I suppose?" The question was rather wistful. Peel seemed to be at loose ends this morning.

"Thanks, no. I'll run down there and have a look."

"Righto. See you later on perhaps."

As Henry walked away he had a disturbed impression that Peel wanted to detain him, to tell him something, but hadn't the courage. This impression was instantly blotted out by the sight of a short, square man in a brown suit and derby, standing in front of a glass display case in the softly lighted corridor. Even without the black umbrella Henry would have recognized Mr. Hedges, the antique dealer he had found in Link's house. He hurried toward him, but without seeming to see Henry's approach the man slid round the case and vanished. Henry spent some minutes searching for him in various alcoves and corridors and even in the main lobby, but the fellow was gone. He was too good at this sort of thing to be an amateur.

On his way to the subway Henry purchased a box of pepper and some dark blue yarn. On the Lexington Avenue express, to the amusement of some of the more conscious passengers, he wound the yarn into a ball.

It was after eleven when he entered the visitors' gallery in the Stock Exchange and looked over the crowd for a familiar hat. There was Miss Ada, peering down at the buzzing floor, her knitting bag held firmly against the rail in both hands.

"Hi, there," Henry said, squeezing in beside her.

Miss Ada jerked away, looked at him coldly, unbent a little when she recognized him. "You are an abrupt young man, Mr. Bryce. How did you find me?"

"Your cousin, Mr. Peel," Henry said, turning his attention to the frenzied men below who tore hither and yon with scraps of colored paper, seized phones, wrote messages, waved arms, and generally appeared to enjoy a special form of insanity.

"You know I've never been here before," Henry told Miss Ada. "It's quite a place. They're almost as crazy as decorators."

A bald man with a genial face looked up from the floor and waved at Miss Ada.

"You've got a friend down there."

"He's been rather cheeky for some time," she told him, not displeased.

A crowd of visitors on a tour pressed them tightly against the rail. Henry didn't know quite how he was going to manage what he wanted to do, but he knew he had to try something soon, before Miss Ada decided to leave.

"Look over there," he cried, pointing into the crowd at her right. "There's a fellow looks exactly like Roy Palling!"

Miss Ada's mouth tightened, showing her resistance to any such idea, but her eyes followed his finger.

Henry jostled her violently, spilled the pepper onto the ledge in front of them. "Sorry," he said, "someone pushed me."

Miss Ada sneezed. The sound was frightening. Several people withdrew from their immediate vicinity. Miss Ada sneezed again and dropped the knitting bag. Henry bent down, made a job of recovering it for her, sneezed himself, managed to remove her ball of yarn and substitute the one he had made on the subway. He returned the knitting bag.

"Thank you," Miss Ada said stiffly. "I believe I've been here long enough."

Henry followed her to the elevator. She seemed less friendly.

"That was the loudest sneeze ever heard in the Stock Exchange," Henry remarked. "U.S. Steel dropped two points."

Miss Ada regarded him coldly.

In the street she announced that they would take a cab. She included Henry in her party as a guard includes a prisoner.

Settled in the cab, she put her large brown-gloved hand into the ample pocket of her loose tweed coat and pulled out a small revolver. This instrument she pointed in a somewhat disturbing manner at Henry's chest.

"I'll take back my yarn, Mr. Bryce," she said.

"Yarn?" Henry repeated stupidly.

"The yarn you so clumsily removed from my knitting bag. Positively childish."

"I don't know what you're driving at, Miss Ada."

"Come. I am not a particularly patient woman." She shifted the gun closer to Henry's shirt buttons. The driver looked round.

"No shootin' in this cab," he said. "That goes for everybody, men or women, old or young. You hear me, lady?"

"I do not need your advice, my good man," Miss Ada retorted. "Tend to your driving and I shall tend to my shooting."

He pulled into the curb in front of a Fanny Farmer candy store, turned to face her. "I don't like to get rough, ma'am, but if you don't put up that gun I'm gonna throw you out of my cab."

Another taxi came alongside, passed them slowly. Miss Ada was facing this other cab as she held the gun against Henry. Her expression suffered a sharp change, and the gun muzzle dropped.

Henry seized the door handle and was out of the cab before she could readjust her firing power.

He dashed round the car and into the candy shop, saw that there was another door giving onto the side street, left by that, and found himself at the Fulton Street entrance to the subway. He spilled some change getting out a dime, didn't stop to pick it up, plunged through the turnstile as a train came in. Miss Ada was no match for him on foot and her cab couldn't follow him into the subway. He sat down, breathing hard, patted his coat pocket where the ball of yarn made a bulge, and tried to look interested in an ad for a product guaranteed to take the smell out of people. He must have revealed signs of mental exertion, because the boy in the pink shirt delivering a good-luck horseshoe of carnations to Al's Bar & Grill held him in focus steadily and suspiciously.

Henry recalled the matter of the saucepan found in the sink the morning after Roy's death. Miss Ada was fond of hot milk and fascinated by the electric stove. The bloody drippings to the pool and Roy's shoe at the bottom sounded like a bit of her doing—

something to confuse the police and make things interesting. Had she wiped her hands or the sword handle on the dish towel?

His nose itched a little, and he rubbed it absently. Funny, he got that smell of aniline suddenly. Must be in his clothes. Or was it? Cautiously he removed the ball of yarn from his pocket and held it to his nose. Aniline, distinctly. Miss Ada had been carrying aniline around in her knitting bag.

The boy with the wreath shifted his attention to someone at the end of the car. Idly, Henry looked there too. He felt a slight constriction in the throat as he recognized the short, square man in the derby hat. He was wiping his forehead with a large handkerchief and the umbrella was absent from his arm. Perhaps he had been in some haste to enter this particular subway train.

They stopped at Fourteenth Street and Henry considered getting off and making a run for it in the crowd. But he felt safer on the train. And anyway, he argued, maybe the little man wasn't following him. Maybe it was just a coincidence. Even if he was following, there was no reason to think he meant any harm. As they slowed for Grand Central Henry pretended no interest in the station. At the last minute he jumped up, wriggled through the cluster of people at the door, and made his way quickly up the stairs. He didn't look round, as he fell into a cab on Forty-second Street, to see if the little man were following him.

When he reached the studio he found Emily alone, placidly finishing the plaid chest.

"Henry, what are you doing up?" she demanded, putting down her brush and getting ready for an argument.

"I think I've got something, if Miss Ada didn't pull a fast one." He found a penknife in the litter on the desk and began cutting open the ball of yarn. It was too slow. "Where are the scissors?"

"What on earth are you doing?" Emily found the scissors and watched him cut the wool. Something fell out, something small, green, and glittering.

Emily snatched it. "My God, Henry, the jewels!" She put the *Daily News* under his operations, and in a moment he had the yarn loosened and a shower of small brilliant gems fell onto the paper.

"Diamonds and emeralds!" Emily's eyes were popping. "Are

they real? Where did you get them? Do we have to turn them over to the police?"

Henry picked up a diamond, held it in his palm so the light caught it. "Pretty, isn't it?"

"I wish they were larger. I've always wanted an emerald as big as a card table."

"Miss Ada had these all the time, in her knitting bag. Pretty clever, wasn't she?"

"I don't believe it. Miss Ada didn't have a thing to do with it. Somebody planted them on her."

"If they did, she was quite aware of the plant. She pulled a gun on me."

Emily didn't believe that either, until they heard a noise behind them, and turned to find Miss Ada covering them with the small revolver. Emily squealed.

"No need to be hysterical," Miss Ada told her severely. "Let me have the gems and I shall not harm you."

"Let's go fifty-fifty," Emily suggested.

Miss Ada didn't have to answer that, because the little man in the brown suit entered the studio and said in a quiet voice, "Miss Birtwistle, kindly put away that plaything."

"Cousin Bertie!" Miss Ada said, putting the gun in her coat pocket. Cousin Bertie scooped up the gems from the *Daily News*.

"He can't have those," Emily cried. "Henry found them."

"He'll take them anyway," Miss Ada said. "That's the government. Bertie is Scotland Yard, in one of its more mediocre personifications."

"Scotland Yard?" Emily was impressed. "Please sit down. Henry, clear off something for the poor man. He must be tired if he's come all that way. Did they know about the jewels and the murder and everything? Isn't that wonderful? They must have electric eyes all over."

"Oh, not so wonderful," Bertie said, liking Emily at once. "It's more or less routine, you know, once one has the trail. That was very nice brandy in your flat, by the way. Thank you. May I use the telephone?"

"Certainly," Emily said. She turned to Miss Ada, and there was something resembling embarrassment on her very open face. "I don't like to be petty, but Miss Birtwistle still has a gun."

"She won't use it," Henry told her, and Cousin Bertie looked unconcerned.

"What makes you think I won't?" Miss Ada countered.

"They can only hang her once, no matter how many times she bumps off people, Henry."

"But she hasn't killed anyone yet."

"No? Who killed Roy, then?"

Henry didn't answer because he was listening to Cousin Bertie. "I've found the material in question, Fisher," he was saying. "Very little remains to be done, then. I should say you ought to take your prisoner, yes. Probably no danger, but time to wind up the business." He looked up as Olivia and her father came in, added quickly, "I say, you'd better come here to the Lentement Studio at once."

Henry said hello to Mr. Peel and Olivia, who were regarding Bertie with astonishment, and ran downstairs to Link's shop. Link was waiting on a female who needed a twelve-foot gilt mirror. "Drop everything," Henry ordered. "Olivia's in a spot."

Link apologized to the woman and they swept her ruffled feathers out of the shop and locked the door. "What's up?" he demanded as they took the stairs two at a time.

"You'll see." Henry looked back and saw Sergeant Fisher coming up behind them. He must have been somewhere quite close when Bertie talked to him, probably down at the Seventeenth Precinct station.

Fisher nodded to the others and spoke to Bertie as if they had been in nursery school together. "Who had the stuff?" he asked. "Let's see it."

"Miss Birtwistle, my cousin, I regret to say." Bertie emptied his pocket on the desk.

Henry saw that Olivia was turning a bad shade of green. He spoke to Fisher in a low voice. "Will it be all right if my friend Simpson takes Mrs. Palling away before you go into the details?"

"I want to know," Olivia said in a small voice.

"You'd better go, Olivia," her father said kindly. "It's a distressing business."

"I shall stay." She leaned slightly against a dusty iron eagle on a pedestal. Link stood beside her, baffled.

"Anyway, your father did it for you," Henry told her, trying to be a comfort. He succeeded in making two large tears roll down her face.

"And very stupid of him too," Miss Ada snapped. She was standing quite close to George Peel, and Henry saw the gun pass from her coat pocket to his hand. Fisher saw it, too, and acquired it.

Link asked to see the weapon. "It's one of my guns," he said, surprised. "How did you get hold of this, Miss Birtwistle?"

"You were busy with a customer. The gun was on the glass case. Very simple."

Mr. Peel smiled dismally. "I shouldn't have the courage to shoot myself, in any case. I'm terribly sorry about all this, Olivia, my dear. I meant to help you, but it became so very involved. Roy discovered that I was attempting to remove a part of my fortune to this country."

"But why did you want your money over here instead of in England?" Emily asked.

"Death duties," he said.

Henry explained. "Inheritance taxes. They practically wipe out an estate. Isn't that so, Mr. Peel?"

"Quite. Very discouraging, when one has managed to accumulate a little something for one's children. I wanted Olivia to be comfortable when I died. There was an added advantage. If the money were invested for her in this country, Roy could not easily locate and spend it. When Jerome came to me with his proposition, I was weak enough to accept. I turned a good portion of my property into easily concealed assets—diamonds and emeralds. These I was to give to Mr. and Mrs. Bryce, sewn into a pair of gilt epaulets which Vittorio had asked them to bring back for him. It became apparent that Roy suspected, so I had to find some other article in which to conceal the gems. I hit on the royal trousers, to which Mrs. Bryce had taken a fancy."

At that moment Alfredo Vittorio came bounding in, his stomach several inches in advance. "Emily darling," he cried. Then he saw the gems, and Sergeant Fisher. He turned an interesting purple and backed toward the door. "Sorry," he murmured. "Don't let me interrupt. I'll see you, Emily dear."

"Please stay, Mr. Vittorio," Fisher commanded.

Alfredo gurgled and sank onto the pink satin sofa.

"What was the plan, Mr. Peel," Fisher continued, "once you had these jewels in the United States?"

"Vittorio, I was informed, would know how to dispose of them." Peel didn't look at Alfredo, who was gasping on the hook.

"But why didn't you tell Vittorio the gems were here in our studio, in Charlie's pants, so he could come and get them?" Henry asked. "You saw Vittorio twice before the murder."

Alfredo was waiting for the answer.

"Vittorio did not know," Mr. Peel explained, "that I was the man whose property was being—transferred. Jerome had told him only that the money was to be deposited in Olivia's name. I thought it much the safest course not to communicate immediately with Vittorio. Roy was alert to every move I made. After Roy's death I hoped I could locate the gems and carry out my original intention. With Roy out of the picture, so to speak, no one knew what I was doing, except Jerome, on whom I could rely since he was equally in the thing."

"I knew what you were doing," Miss Ada reminded him.

"But you'd have helped me." Peel smiled at her sadly. "I hoped we could make it appear that Roy had been in some sort of un-wholesome business."

"Did you think," Henry asked, "that Vittorio had the gems when you searched his studio?"

Emily cut in. "You mean it was Mr. Peel who threw things at me in Alfredo's studio?"

"Not only that," Henry agreed, "but I'm quite sure Mr. Peel followed you home and knocked you out in our hall. Right?"

Peel nodded. "I'm terribly sorry, Emily, my dear. If there had been any other way—"

"Oh, it's nothing," Emily told him. "At least I wasn't on your exterminating list." She turned to Miss Birtwistle. "I still don't get it. How did you happen to have the diamonds, Miss Ada?"

"I took them from those ridiculous royal pants on the plane. It was obvious Roy knew what was going on. If he could find the gems he would appropriate them, one could be certain. I did not believe he could find them in my knitting bag. I was right, no one

knew they were there until today. I'm sure Bertie didn't know I
had them, did you, Bertie?"

"Oh, we knew you had them," he said, "but we didn't know
where."

Miss Ada sniffed. "They always pretend to be all-wise, these
Yard men."

Emily shrugged. "It just goes to show you might get rid of a
husband once in a while, but you can't get rid of the government."

Link wanted to know why Henry had fixed on Mr. Peel as Roy's
murderer.

"Easy, wasn't it, Bryce?" Fisher taunted. "With a mind like his
you can figure these things out over a highball."

Henry smiled. "It took me a little longer than that, Sergeant. I
figured the smuggling could have been done by any one of the
four. If there was smuggling. But Mr. Peel had recently sold his
business and other properties. He had money to leave to Olivia,
and I knew about the devastating taxes. When it came to killing
Roy, a sword seemed a clumsy and uncertain weapon for a woman.
It wasn't a well-planned weapon for anyone. It seemed to me Roy
had been killed in sudden anger. He had possibly threatened his
killer. Olivia, we were reasonably certain, had been drugged and
had slept through the whole thing. Miss Ada, while perfectly capable of doing away with a loathsome character like Roy, seemed
to me too much of a philosopher to bother. But she was alert to
what was going on. She came out, saw Roy dead, and proceeded
to mess up the evidence by heating some milk for herself, carrying
the dripping sword across the living room and porch, wiping her
bloody hands on the dish towel—"

"Indeed not," Miss Ada corrected him sharply. "I wrapped the
handle of the sword in the dish towel. Then I placed the coffeepot
on the hearth, emptied Roy's pockets, removed his boots and socks,
and threw one boot into the swimming pool." She gave Fisher a
complacent smile.

Link put in a word. "If Mr. Peel didn't plan to kill Palling, as
you say, Henry, then why did he put something in Olivia's wine to
make her sleep through the unpleasantness?"

"I didn't do that," Peel said promptly.

"Perhaps Palling drugged the madeira," Henry suggested, "so

that he could talk to Mr. Peel undisturbed."

Peel nodded. "As soon as the others had gone to bed he opened fire. Told me he knew what I had done. I offered him a substantial sum if he would divorce Olivia and leave us both in peace. He laughed. Roy had a most irritating laugh. Said he had no quarrel with Olivia. He wanted the money and my daughter."

"I thought Palling was too drunk on Saturday night to know what was going on," Link objected.

Peel said that had been a good performance. "He knew Olivia would leave us if he appeared a bit disgusting. She left and Roy began to taunt me."

"Taunt?" Emily repeated, turning over her vocabulary.

"Needle," Miss Ada told her. "Roy was a skillful needler—but perhaps you didn't know?"

"We heard him going over Olivia the first night we were in the Royal Rajah."

Mr. Peel went on. "He repeated a ridiculous number of times that I was now a criminal. He threatened me with exposure."

"It seems to me, George," Miss Ada said practically, "that exposure for smuggling would have been preferable to exposure for murder."

He regarded her good-naturedly. "Admittedly, Cousin Ada. I'm afraid I lost my temper. I had put up with Roy—we all had—for a good long while, and suddenly I couldn't put up with him any longer. I had to shut him up somehow."

"You shut him up," Emily agreed. "But with all that blood pouring around the living room, weren't you scared when you got through?"

"I was a bit nervous." Peel gave Emily a faint smile. "But I hoped, as you say over here, to get away with it."

"Why?" Fisher inquired.

"I had an erroneous idea, gained from your pictures, that murder was such a common occurrence here that you didn't bother a great deal. People seemed to be obliterated in the most casual manner."

"I could have corrected that impression," Miss Ada said sternly. "The killing goes on, of course, but frequently they endeavor to nail the culprit."

"I knew I was wrong as soon as I saw Sergeant Fisher," Peel admitted. He turned to Bertie, sitting there with his derby on his knees. "I don't see how you came into it, Bertie."

"Neither do I," Miss Ada admitted. "He's never been what one would call brainy."

Bertie bowed in her direction. "Jerome had done this sort of thing before. Not apprehended, but we were suspicious. When the Yard learned he had once again imported American decorators for a wealthy gentleman, we looked around a bit. Then we got an inquiry about Jerome from the police here, and we were hot on the scent. I came over at once, talked to Sergeant Fisher, and received permission to carry on in any manner I saw fit."

"Even to sampling the liquor everywhere you went," Miss Ada said scornfully.

"One is entitled to one's small pleasures. And I discovered why Olivia had been so unconcerned about her husband during the night. An important fact, really."

"Who put the ad in the *Times?*" Henry demanded.

"I did," Peel told him. "I wanted to get in touch with Marie Dennis. I felt she might have the gems. I received no reply."

"But I answered," Henry said. "And Miss Ada met me behind the library. I thought I saw you, Mr. Peel, on a bench a little way off."

"You did. I followed Cousin Ada. She seemed so full of business that I was curious."

"I was there too," Olivia told him with an effort. "I knew my father had placed an advertisement for Marie. When I went to the *Times* office to see if I could intercept the reply Cousin Ada was already there. I waited until she came out with a letter, pretended to be passing, and joined her. I tried to see the letter, but she was very cautious with it. Finally I had to leave her—I was already late for a luncheon engagement." She looked apologetically at Link. "Naturally when Cousin Ada left the hotel that evening, I followed her."

"Why didn't you tell me you had the gems, Cousin Ada?" Peel asked her without any bitterness.

"They were quite safe with me, George. And I didn't know what outrageous thing you might do."

"I'd like to know who took the heels off my shoes in the Royal Rajah," Emily said.

Mr. Peel had not done so, neither had Miss Ada. Therefore it must have been Roy. "Probably," Henry reflected, "he picked up the package containing the epaulets which Emily had left in the drawing room, discovered the jewels were not in them, and tried Emily's heels." He looked severely at Miss Ada. "I still feel annoyed about the aniline oil on my paintbrush."

"I'm sorry, Henry," she said. "I had no idea it would make you really ill. I wanted you to be concerned over yourself so that you wouldn't go on thinking about poor George."

"And all the time Miss Ada kept saying people ought to be inactive after a murder," Emily remarked. "Foxy, weren't you?"

Fisher took Mr. Peel's arm. "We'll be on our way, if you don't mind. You, too, Vittorio—we want a statement."

Bertie scooped up the jewels, took Alfredo's arm, and they went out with their prey. Olivia started to follow, but Link held onto her.

"You'd better stay here," he said gently. "We'll have to get lawyers and tend to things."

"Do you think there's any chance for him?"

"There were extenuating circumstances," Henry ventured.

"Yes," Emily agreed brightly, "and he's such a nice man. They wouldn't be mean to him."

"He is still a murderer," Miss Ada reminded them. "So unnecessary too. But then George never had much sense, except for making money. Soft, that's his trouble."

Olivia looked miserably from one to the other. "They may sentence him to death."

"I think not, Olivia," Miss Ada said. "But suppose they do? George accomplished what he was capable of—he provided for you and he disposed of Roy. I could never understand all this fuss about longevity."

Link smiled. "That's all very well when you have longevity, isn't it, Miss Ada?"

"I shouldn't have minded dying at twenty."

"Oh, but think what you'd have missed," Emily protested.

"Five wars and the Duchess of Windsor."

THE END

If you enjoyed *The Green Plaid Pants*, ask your bookseller for a copy of Emily and Henry's first case, *The Gun in Daniel Webster's Bust* (0-915230-74-7, $14.95). The Rue Morgue intends to publish all four titles in this series as well as those featuring the Rev. Buell plus several standalones. Details on The Rue Morgue may be found on the next page.

About the Rue Morgue Press

"Rue Morgue Press is the old-mystery lover's best friend, reprinting high quality books from the 1930s and '40s."
—*Ellery Queen's Mystery Magazine*

Since 1997, the Rue Morgue Press has reprinted scores of traditional mysteries, the kind of books that were the hallmark of the Golden Age of detective fiction. Authors reprinted or to be reprinted by the Rue Morgue include Dorothy Bowers, Joanna Cannan, Glyn Carr, Torrey Chanslor, Clyde B. Clason, Joan Coggin, Manning Coles, Lucy Cores, Frances Crane, Norbert Davis, Elizabeth Dean, Constance & Gwenyth Little, Marlys Millhiser, James Norman, Stuart Palmer, Craig Rice, Kelley Roos, Charlotte Murray Russell, Maureen Sarsfield, and Juanita Sheridan.

To suggest titles or to receive a catalog of Rue Morgue Press books write P.O. Box 4119, Boulder, CO 80306, telephone 800-699-6214, or check out our website, www.ruemorguepress.com, which lists complete descriptions of all of our titles, along with lengthy biographies of our writers.